"The Miss Marple–like Raisin is a refreshingly sensible, wonderfully eccentric, thoroughly likable heroine . . . a must for cozy fans." —*Booklist*

SOMETHING BORROWED, SOMEONE DEAD

"In [this] lively mystery . . . Agatha displays a wit and sharp tongue that will continue to please her many fans." —*Publishers Weekly*

"M.C. Beaton is one of my favorite cozy authors, and her latest installment will not disappoint her fans. There's just something about the characters and reading the books makes me feel like I'm visiting old friends." —Criminal Element

"Just like its predecessors, [*Something Borrowed, Someone Dead*] provides plenty of twists and turns to keep the reader guessing." —Bookreporter.com

HISS AND HERS

"As always, M. C. Beaton presents us with an Agatha Raisin who manages to infuriate, amuse, and solicit our deepest sympathies as we watch her blunder her way boldly through another murder mystery." —Bookreporter

"Agatha continues looking for love in the most unlikely places. In spite of her inability to learn from past mistakes, one can't help but root for her to solve the mystery and, at the same time, find a man who will love her truly and deeply just the way she is."

—Criminal Element

AS THE PIG TURNS

"Beaton has written a pleasantly twisty cozy for the holidays."

—*RT Book Reviews*

"It's been said of Agatha Christie that she's given more pleasure in bed than any other woman, but M.C. Beaton is matching her as a prolific purveyor of cozy whodunits perfect for pre-lights out reading . . . like *Midsomer Murders* with wit and a bit of edge."

—*The Daily Telegraph* (UK)

"Hilarious . . . Beaton's legion of fans will most definitely enjoy her latest Agatha Raisin mystery, *As the Pig Turns*. Newcomers to the series will be pleasantly surprised by this unique cozy." —*Gumshoe Reviews*

"Who but Agatha Raisin could spot such an unusual method of disposing of a body?"

—*Kirkus Reviews*

"Take two fine old English traditions—the village fete and death by poison—and you have a clever tale . . . featuring irascible, lovable Agatha Raisin. *A Spoonful of Poison* will go down just fine."

—Richmond Times-Dispatch

"Beaton's sly humor enhances the cozy-style plotting, while updates on Agatha's . . . romantic travails are as delightful as ever. The open-ended resolution points to more madcap mayhem to come."   —*Publishers Weekly*

KISSING CHRISTMAS GOODBYE

"Agatha Raisin is still at the top of her game . . . in her most challenging case yet."   —*Publishers Weekly*

"Beaton, the reigning queen of the cozies, adds an English manor house and a Christmas theme to her usual Cotswold village setting, upping the comfiness factor even higher."   —*Booklist*

LOVE, LIES AND LIQUOR

"Another highly satisfying Beaton cozy, this one is long on the kind of social comedy that uses character, plot, and atmosphere to produce the laughter."

—Booklist

Also by M. C. Beaton

Something Borrowed, Someone Dead

An Agatha Raisin Mystery

M. C. BEATON

St. Martin's Paperbacks

This is a work of fiction. All of the characters, organizations, and events portrayed in this novel are either products of the author's imagination or are used fictitiously.

SOMETHING BORROWED, SOMEONE DEAD

Copyright © 2013 by M.C. Beaton.
Excerpt from *The Blood of an Englishman* copyright © 2014 by M.C. Beaton.

For information address St. Martin's Press, 175 Fifth Avenue, New York, N.Y. 10010.

EAN: 978-1-250-04756-4

Printed in the United States of America

Minotaur hardcover edition / September 2013
St. Martin's Paperbacks edition / July 2014

St. Martin's Paperbacks are published by St. Martin's Press, 175 Fifth Avenue, New York, NY 10010.

10 9 8 7 6 5 4 3 2 1

To the Golden Voice of Scotland,
Grant Mackintosh, and Desmond King,
with affection

Chapter One

The recession was biting deeper into private detective Agatha Raisin's finances. The bread-and-butter work of her agency, the divorces, missing teenagers, even missing dogs and cats, was drying up as people preferred to go to the police for free help, and men and women in unhappy marriages opted to wait before paying Agatha to find proof of evidence for divorce.

Her agency staff consisted of two young people, Toni Gilmour and Simon Black, as well as retired policeman, Patrick Mulligan, elderly Phil Marshall, and secretary Mrs. Freedman.

Despite the hard times, Agatha could not bring herself to lay any of them off. She spent more time at her cottage in the village of Carsely in the Cotswolds, smoking, drinking gin and tonic and playing with her cats, Hodge and Boswell. Her ex-husband, James Lacey, who had the cottage next door, wrote travel books and was often absent, her police detective, Bill Wong, was too busy to call, and her other friend, Sir Charles Fraith, had not called on her for over a month.

So one sunny morning, instead of going into the office, she trudged up the road to the vicarage to pay a call on her closest friend, Mrs. Bloxby, the vicar's wife. The two women were in sharp contrast. Mrs. Bloxby wore old-fashioned "lady" clothes: drooping skirts and blouses in summer and washed-out woollens in winter. She had brown hair, mild eyes, and very beautiful hands. Agatha had bearlike eyes in a round face. She had very good skin and glossy brown hair worn short. Her figure was quite good apart from a rather thick waistline and her legs were excellent.

"Come in, Mrs. Raisin," she said. "I've just made some coffee. We can have it in the garden." Both women addressed each other by their second names, a practise once used by the now defunct Ladies Society.

Agatha sat in a chair in the sunny vicarage garden. Behind the garden wall lay the church graveyard, old mossy tombstones reminding one detective in her early fifties that life was fleeting.

Mrs. Bloxby came out to join her, carrying a tray with the coffee and a plate of Eccles cakes.

"I made these this morning," said the vicar's wife.

"I'd love one but I can't," said Agatha gloomily. "All this inactivity is going straight to my waistline. Oh, what the hell!"

She picked up a cake and bit into it.

Mrs. Bloxby looked at her friend anxiously. She felt she could hardly pray to God to send down a case for Agatha, as that possibly would involve a lot of misery for some people. Her husband often complained that people shouldn't pray for specifics, but, thought Mrs. Bloxby, there was often comfort in trying because the answer could be "no" but, on the other hand, something might happen.

Scotland Yard once claimed that some people are murderees. Mrs. Bloxby could not have imagined that in a village not far away from Carsely was a widow who would cause such hatred as to spur someone to murder her and give Agatha Raisin a new case.

Mrs. Gloria French lived in the village of Piddlebury, a charming place of old cottages, nestling in the

Cotswold hills. She was a jolly widow with dyed blond hair, rosy cheeks and a raucous laugh. The perpetual smile on her wide mouth never quite reached her prominent pale blue eyes. She had recently moved to the Cotswolds from London and had thrown herself into village life with great energy. She baked cakes for the Women's Institute. She delivered the *Church Times*. She organised parties to raise money to repair the old church. In short, she seemed indefatigable.

Gloria's cottage had a thatched roof and latticed windows. The latticed windows were a recent addition, Gloria thinking that plain glass was not, well, *cottagey* enough. Nestling among the profusion of flowers in her garden were plastic gnomes.

Inside, the living room and kitchen were decorated with many copper pans and fake horse brasses. Some bad watercolours hung on the walls, Gloria being an enthusiastic amateur artist. "If you are very good," she was fond of saying, "I will give you one of my pictures," but the ungrateful villagers hoped they were never going to be considered good enough.

She favoured tight dresses of shiny material over a body stocking, giving her figure a sausage-like appearance. Gloria was determined to marry again. She ruthlessly pursued the few eligible men in the village with the exception of Jerry Tarrant, head of the parish council, who had complained about the amount of scent she wore by saying, "We're supposed to get a whiff as we walk past you, not when we drive past you at sixty miles an hour," for Gloria sprayed herself daily from top to bottom in L'Air Du Temps.

Everyone hoped she would settle down, as they were used to newcomers trying to take over and immersing themselves in what they believed was village life.

The vicar, Guy Enderbury, however, was delighted with her efforts. Not only had Gloria raised a healthy sum of money for the church restoration but also she read to the elderly and took them on shopping trips.

He found it hard to understand why she was becoming so unpopular, and appealed to his wife, Clarice.

Said Clarice, "She's pushy, but it's not only that. She borrows things and doesn't give them back. When people ask for their belongings, she swears blind the items are her own property."

Such was the case. The items were hardly ever very expensive, a teapot here, a set of knives there, things like that.

Had she not been such a formidable character, people would have stopped lending her things, but when she loomed up on their doorsteps, they often weakly gave in, just wanting to be rid of her.

As Agatha was drinking coffee with Mrs. Bloxby, Gloria applied another slash of red lipstick to her large mouth and headed for the cottage of Peter Suncliff. Peter was a retired engineer and a widower. He was a tall powerful man in his early sixties with a good head of white hair and a craggy face. Gloria considered him top of her list as husband material.

He opened the door and looked down at Gloria. "What?" he demanded curtly.

"The vicar's calling round and I am out of sherry," said Gloria. She tried to move past him, into his cottage, but he barred the way. "I wondered if I could borrow a bottle."

"There's no need for that," said Peter. "The village store is still open, or had you forgotten? They sell sherry. Or had you forgotten that as well?" And, with that, he slammed the door in her face.

Gloria turned away, baffled. Then she thought he was probably shy and was frightened of betraying his real feelings.

She was just leaving when she was accosted by Jenny Soper. Jenny was also a widow, small and dainty, with a good figure and a round face with dimples under a head of curly black hair. "Oh, Gloria," she said. "Do you remember you borrowed a bag of flour from me? Do you mind replacing it?"

"What? Oh, that? What's a bag of flour between friends?"

"We are not friends," said Jenny.

Gloria ignored her and strode on to the village stores. Jenny followed her. "I'm telling you," shouted Jenny, "I want you to replace that bag of flour. Buy one now and give it to me."

"No, I haven't enough money on me at the moment," said Gloria. "Really, Jenny! You're all flushed. What a lot of fuss over a mere bag of flour."

"You're a greedy cow!" said Jenny. "I wish someone would kill you!" She stomped off.

Gloria beamed round at the startled villagers in the shop. "Dear Jenny," she said, shaking her head. "But there you are, the menopause takes women in odd ways."

"Her be too young," said old Mrs. Tripp. "Menopause, indeed. And don't you come reading to me no more. Hear?"

Gloria looked at her, aghast. All the hours she had spent reading to that smelly old woman. "What's more," said Mrs. Tripp, shuffling forward with the aid of two sticks, "you're long past the change yourself, I does reckon."

Gloria could hardly believe her ears. She was in her early fifties and prided herself on looking at least ten years younger.

She smiled at the watching villagers. "The heat does seem to be getting to everyone this morning."

They all turned their backs on her. Gloria was not

sensitive, but even such as she felt an air of menace around her, a sort of menace that was as old as the Cotswold hills.

Unlike most Cotswold villages these days, which abound with outsiders, nearly all of the residents were from families who had lived in Piddlebury for generations.

Gloria hurriedly purchased a bottle of the cheapest sherry she could find and made her way home.

The phone was ringing when she entered her cottage and she rushed to answer it.

It was the vicar. "My dear Mrs. French," he said, "I am afraid I cannot join you this morning. Something has come up."

"What?" demanded Gloria.

"Parish business."

"What kind of parish business?"

Then clear as a bell, she could hear the vicar's wife shouting, "Have you managed to put her off?"

"I'll tell you next time I see you," said Guy Enderbury. "Got to rush."

And then he rang off.

Gloria slowly replaced the receiver. She needed a drink. But not this filthy cheap sherry. She had the very thing down in the cellar. She went down the narrow stairs. On the floor lay a crate containing a few bottles of elderberry wine. She had organised the refreshments at a Bring & Buy sale at the church hall a month ago. A local farmer's wife, Mrs. Ada White, had contributed the wine to be sold. Gloria, knowing the homemade wine to be especially good, had stolen the crate that Ada had put under the table as a reserve. One bottle at the corner of the crate had a printed label on it she had not noticed before. It read: VERY SPECIAL.

That'll do, thought Gloria. She lifted out a bottle and took it upstairs.

Pouring a large glass, she swallowed a greedy gulp and then gasped. She thought it must have gone off. Her body was racked with convulsions and she vomited violently. Then her bowels gave. She tried to get out of her armchair and reach the phone. But when she stood up, her legs gave out from under her and she fell to the ground. Her vision blurred and the room grew dark as she dragged herself into her small hallway. She made one last effort to raise herself up, but she slipped into a coma.

Three hours later, Jenny met Peter Suncliff in the main street. The village was really only made up of this one street. There were only two lanes leading off it. The cottages fronted straight onto the street without gardens.

"How are you this morning, Jenny?" asked Peter.

"Still angry. That wretched French woman. She borrowed a bag of flour from me and won't give one back. She goes round the village, borrowing one thing or another, except it isn't borrowing, it's stealing. She never gives anything back. I mean, it's only a bag of flour but someone has to stand up to her."

"I'll come with you," said Peter, who had a soft spot for pretty Jenny.

They walked together to Gloria's cottage and rang the bell. Mrs. Ada White stopped beside them, a shopping basket over her arm. "She often doesn't answer," she said. "I know she stole my elderberry wine but when I went to see her, she wouldn't answer the door although I'd seen her going in a few minutes before I rang the bell."

"Let's just leave it," said Jenny.

"No. It's time she got a real lecture." Peter bent down and shouted through the letterbox. "Open up! We know you're in there."

Then he straightened up, a worried frown on his face. "What's up?" asked Jenny.

He didn't answer but bent down again and this time looked through the letterbox.

He tried the door but it was locked. "Call for an ambulance, Jenny," he said. "She's had a turn. I'll try to break in."

The front door had a glass panel. While Jenny dialled

999 on her mobile, Peter picked up a stone from the street and smashed the glass of the door. He gingerly put his arm through the hole he had made, found the lock and opened it.

Gloria's make-up stood out starkly against the clay of her face. He felt for a pulse but could not find one.

The ambulance took half an hour to arrive. People began to gather outside the cottages.

Two paramedics rushed in while Peter and Jenny waited nervously outside.

One of the paramedics came outside and said, "We've called the police."

"Why?" asked Peter.

"It looks like poisoning. Nothing must be touched."

Agatha read about it the following day in a local newspaper. Her interest quickened and then died. She could not afford to investigate any case where she could not earn any money.

At the week-end, she was morosely looking at her garden, feeling that she should try to weed some of the flowerbeds, and deciding to sit down and have a gin and tonic and a cigarette instead, when her doorbell rang.

When she opened the door, she found her friend Detective Sergeant Bill Wong on the doorstep. "Come in!" cried Agatha. "I thought all my friends had forgotten me."

"Been very busy," said Bill.

Bill Wong had been Agatha's first friend when she had newly arrived to stay in the Cotswolds. He was the product of a Chinese father and a Gloucestershire mother. He had a round face and almond-shaped eyes and a pleasant local accent.

"Drink?" suggested Agatha, leading the way into the garden where her two cats, Hodge and Boswell, chased shadows across the shaggy lawn.

"Too early for me and too early for you," said Bill, settling himself down in a garden chair. The cats rushed to give him a welcome.

"It's eleven o' clock," snapped Agatha, "and the pubs are open. Don't be a Puritan."

"I'll have a coffee."

When Agatha returned with a mug of coffee, it was to find that Hodge had draped himself around Bill's neck while Boswell lay purring on his lap. Agatha looked sourly at the scene. Her cats only seemed glad to see her when it was feeding time.

"What's new?" she asked, sitting down beside him.

"An odd case over at Piddlebury."

"Oh, the suspected poisoning. Is it poisoning?"

"Seems like it. Still waiting for the results of the

autopsy. A preliminary search shows that she had been drinking elderberry wine just before she died."

"Some of that homemade stuff is enough to poison anyone," remarked Agatha.

"But there is no sign of a glass or a bottle. There are about four bottles of the stuff in a crate in the cellar. They've been taken away for analysis. The back door of the cottage was unlocked. Someone must have got in and removed the evidence."

"Any suspects?"

"None so far. She appears to have been the saint of the village, raising money for the church and doing good works all round."

"Give it time," said Agatha cynically. "At first, no one will speak ill of the dead. Was she rich?"

"Very comfortably off. Her house is worth at least half a million. She had a healthy amount of stock shares and a large bank balance. Her husband was owner of a company which manufactured Crispy Crisps, potato chips in all kinds of flavours."

"So who inherits?"

"There's a son and daughter. But they both have alibis and were estranged from mother. Son Wayne was managing director of Crispy Crisps but when her husband died, Gloria sold off the whole business and left him without a job."

"Aha!"

"Aha, nothing," said Bill gloomily. "He's got a good job as managing director of a rival company, Neat Nibbles. And he's only twenty-nine. On the day of her death, he was seen around the factory by hundreds of people."

"What about the daughter?"

"Tracey Altrop is married to a wealthy farmer. On the morning of the murder she was down at the church in the village of Ancombe, doing the flowers."

"Could someone have poisoned one of the bottles, knowing she would get around to drinking it eventually?"

"We've thought of that. The wine was made by Mrs. Ada White. Gloria nicked it from a Bring & Buy sale at the church a week ago. When challenged, Gloria swore blind she hadn't seen it."

"So there's a crack in her impeccable do-good character," said Agatha. "If she stole the wine, maybe she stole other things."

Bill smiled. "Wish you were on the case?"

"It would be more interesting than the rubbish I've got to deal with," said Agatha. "I wish someone would pay me to look into it."

"Cheer up. The son and daughter are rich. Maybe they'll ask for your help."

A week went by and Agatha had almost forgotten about the case when she received a visit in her office from Jerry Tarrant, head of the Piddlebury parish council. He was an incredibly neat-looking man, wearing a blue shirt and silk tie with jeans which had been pressed into knife-edged creases over a pair of gleaming white trainers. He looked as if he had tried to dress casually but couldn't quite make it. His thin brown hair was combed in strips over a bald patch on his head. His features were small: small brown eyes, small button of a nose and a little mouth.

He introduced himself, sitting down opposite Agatha and arranging the creases in his jeans so that they fell vertically. He introduced himself. Agatha brightened and slammed shut a folder of missing pets.

"How can I help you?" she asked. "Is it about the recent murder in your village?"

"It is indeed." His voice was high and fluting. "Normally we would leave matters to the police, but we need the case solved quickly. We have been, up till now, a happy village. Now, everyone seems to suspect everyone else."

"What kind of person was Gloria French?" asked Agatha. "And please do speak ill of the dead if necessary."

"She bought a house in the village a year ago and at first she seemed an exemplary woman. She read to the elderly and did their shopping for them, she raised money to restore the church, things like that. And then she developed a habit of borrowing things and refusing to give them back. Never anything very valuable, wine-glasses for a party she was giving, scissors, a teapot and all sorts of bits and pieces. On her last day, she tried to borrow a bottle of sherry from one of the villagers."

"Who will fund this?" asked Agatha. "My rates are quite high."

"I shall pay your rates myself," said Jerry. "I want my tranquil village back. If you discover the identity of the murderer, I will pay you a generous bonus. I am not a poor man."

Agatha told Mrs. Freedman to draw up a contract. After she had finished discussing her fee and expenses, Agatha asked, "Have you any idea who might have committed this murder?"

"We do not have incomers in our village. Well, Gloria was one and Peter Suncliff, a retired engineer, the other. But I can't think of anyone else."

"But they are accusing each other. Is one person the favourite?"

"There is one ridiculous suggestion from some that it might be Jenny Soper, because Jenny was heard threatening to kill her. But Jenny is a sweet little thing and wouldn't harm a fly."

"I have never been to Piddlebury," said Agatha. "What's it like?"

"Very small. More of a hamlet than a village. There's one main street with a church at one end and a pub at the other."

At that moment, Toni Gilmour walked into the office. With old-fashioned courtesy, Jerry jumped to his feet. Agatha introduced him and said that Toni would be one of her staff helping with the investigation.

Toni was young and beautiful with blond hair, wide blue eyes and a perfect figure. Jerry beamed at her. Men always beamed at Toni, reflected Agatha with a little sour stab of jealousy. I probably won't live long enough to see her lose her looks, she thought miserably, and immediately wanted a cigarette. But she fought against the urge. She was, once more, desperately trying to give up.

Jerry opened a briefcase and pulled out a selection of photographs. "These were taken at the last church fete," he said. "I have written the names on the back. I have also here a typed list of the names of most of the villagers and a short description of each person."

A man after my own heart, thought Agatha.

"When do you plan to start?" asked Jerry.

"Oh, I think we can begin today," said Agatha, planning to inflict the folder of lost pets on Simon Black.

Jerry signed the contract and took his leave. Five minutes later, Patrick Mulligan walked in. Agatha thought, not for the first time, that Patrick's appearance always seemed to scream policeman, from his lugubrious face to his grey suit and highly polished black shoes.

After she had briefed Patrick and told him to get in touch with some of his old police contacts to find out what he could about the case, she asked, "Any idea yet what poisoned her?"

"Rhubarb."

"Rhubarb! But I had rhubarb tart last week and I'm fine."

"Rhubarb leaves are highly poisonous, particularly when they're cooked up with soda. It turns out she had a weak heart or she might just have survived. I was talking to an old pal down at police headquarters about it. He said the kitchen door at the back was unlocked because someone came in and took the bottle and glass away. There were bottles of the wine in a crate in the cellar. There were footprints going down to the cellar, some appear to be from Gloria herself and then a set of larger prints, and they were recent footprints. So what is puzzling the police is that although it looks as if the murderer just popped a bottle of the poisoned stuff in with the others and sat back and waited, how would the murderer know that Gloria would drink out of that bottle and when, so as to be on hand to remove the evidence? Also the vicar says that Gloria often entertained him, supplying the cheapest drink possible, and recently she had offered him elderberry wine. It looks as if our murderer didn't care who he or she bumped off as long as one of the people was Gloria."

"Keep at it, Patrick," said Agatha, rapidly taking notes. "Toni and I will pop over there and suss the place out."

As Agatha and Toni got out of Agatha's car in the main street of Piddlebury, Toni thought it looked like a picture postcard. A few thatched houses crouched on either side of the street intermingled with slate-roofed ones of a more recent date, probably Georgian, thought Toni, unlike their Tudor neighbours. The steeple of the church at one end of the village, like one enormous sundial, cast a shadow as the sun moved behind it.

Gloria's cottage was recognisable because of the police tape outside it and the white tent erected over the door.

"Where do we start?" asked Toni.

"The pub," said Agatha. "I'm hungry."

The pub, the Green Man, was a square building of mellow golden Cotswold stone. An old wisteria covered most of the front. The painting of the green man, that ancient fertility symbol, had a singularly evil-looking face with vines sprouting from his nostrils.

Agatha and Toni entered the cool dark bar. "I hope, since this village is not on the tourist map, that they have some real food," whispered Agatha. She approached the bar. "Do you serve lunches?"

The tall thin greying man behind the bar held out his hand. "You'll be the detective ladies Mr. Tarrant was telling us about."

"Yes, that's us," said Agatha. "You are . . . ?"

"Moses Green, owner of this here establishment."

"We're hungry. What do you have?"

He handed Agatha a menu. Agatha looked at it with a sinking heart. Lasagne and chips, egg and chips, sausage and chips, ham and chips, ploughmans and tomato soup. Her face fell.

"Haven't you any real food?"

"Seeing as it's you, you can have a bit of the wife's roast lamb, if you'd like that?"

"Great." They ordered two halves of lager and retreated to a corner table.

"We're the only customers," whispered Toni.

When Moses arrived with their food, Agatha asked, "Is it always as quiet as this?"

"Oh, folks are here but they're out in the garden at the back. The smokers like it there."

Agatha was about to suggest joining them, but realised how hard she was trying to stop smoking, but compromised by saying that they would take their coffee in the garden after they had eaten. After all, she reminded herself, she was here to interview the locals.

The lamb was excellent. After they had finished eating, they walked along a stone-flagged corridor and into the garden at the back. The hum of conversation stopped and the diners turned and looked at them.

"I am Agatha Raisin, private detective," announced Agatha in a loud voice. A loud *hectoring* voice, thought Toni uneasily. "And I am here to investigate the murder of Gloria French. Can any of you help me?"

In that moment, Toni wished that someone of her own age, Simon Black, say, was investigating this case with her. Being with Agatha was like being towed along in the wake of a battleship.

Everyone bent their heads over their food and soon a murmur of conversation rose again. Hands on hips, Agatha viewed them with frustration.

"Let's sit down and have our coffee and I'll take it one table at a time," said Toni. "I think you frighten them."

"I don't frighten people," said Agatha crossly. "People *warm* to me."

"Not this lot," said Toni. "Sit down, drink coffee, have a cigarette and leave it to me."

"You forget who's in charge here," said Agatha crossly.

"Believe me, not for a moment."

"Oh, do your best," said Agatha sulkily.

As Toni approached the nearest table, Agatha opened her file of photographs. Toni was now talking to Peter Suncliff and Jenny Soper. She rather hoped they would give Toni the brush-off, but to her irritation she saw Peter pull out a chair for Toni and soon they were deep in conversation.

Agatha lit a cigarette, the first of the day, and felt her head swim. She cursed under her breath and stubbed it out, frightened by visions of having to walk around with a portable oxygen tank.

To her relief, she saw Toni waving to her. She rose and walked over.

Toni introduced them. "We've been talking about Gloria. They can't help much," she said.

"And I'd help you if I could," said Jenny. "I was heard hoping that someone would kill her. Of course I didn't mean it, but it was infuriating the way she would pretend to borrow things when she had no intention of ever handing them back or paying anyone for what she took. You'll have a difficult job getting anyone else to talk to you. The police have questioned everyone in the village. All that's done is to stir up trouble. Everyone is pointing the finger at everyone else."

"That's the trouble with the police," said Agatha. "They make everyone feel guilty. Don't worry. I'll find this killer if it's the last thing I do."

Agatha was not to know that it would turn out to be nearly the very last thing she did do.

Chapter Two

When they left the pub, Agatha said, "Let's try the vicar. Jerry Tarrant said Gloria did a lot for the church."

The church of St. Edmund's was small, but with its tall steeple pointing up to the summer sky. The vicarage, a pleasant Georgian building, stood beside it.

Agatha rang the bell. The door was opened by a truculent woman with a very red face over which hung wisps of grey hair.

"Mrs. Enderbury?" asked Agatha.

"You want her indoors," said the woman. "I'm just

the help. Visitors!" she yelled into the cool gloom of the vicarage hall behind her.

A tall thin woman emerged from a room off the hall and approached them. "Thank you, Mrs. Pound," she said. The cleaner retreated to the nether regions. The vicar's wife looked at Agatha enquiringly.

Agatha introduced herself and Toni. "Do come in," said Clarice. "Such a hot day. Jerry told us he had employed you." She raised her voice. "Darling! It's the detective lady."

A door in the hall opened and the vicar came out. He was as tall and thin as his wife, with heavy-lidded eyes and a long nose. "I'm just finishing a sermon," he said, after the introductions had been made. "Clarice, why don't you take the ladies into the garden and give them some lemonade and I'll join you shortly."

"Good idea," said his wife. She led the way along a stone-flagged corridor at the end of the hall and out into a sunny garden, crammed with flowers. There was a table on a little terrace overlooking the garden, shaded with an umbrella.

"Do sit down," she urged. "Lemonade?"

"No, thanks," said Agatha. "We've just had lunch in the pub." They sat round the table.

The vicar's wife removed a sun hat, revealing a head of thick red hair, tied up in a knot. Her eyes were very large and green. She had a long face and a small mouth. She was wearing an old print dress and sandals.

"What can you tell us about Gloria French?" asked Agatha.

"She did a lot of good work for the church," said Clarice. "Guy was very grateful to her."

"But what did you think of her? Really think of her?" asked Agatha.

Clarice hesitated. Then, to their surprise, she fished down into her brassiere and produced a crumpled packet of cigarettes and a lighter. She lit a cigarette and watched a puff of smoke drift across the garden.

"We really need to know," said Toni quietly. "There must have been something about her character to make someone want to kill her."

"Well, I suppose in that case . . . She was a cow," said Clarice. "A nasty, bullying woman. Guy said she must be a really good Christian to do so much work to raise funds for the church, but it was all manipulation and control. She even had the cheek to flirt with my husband in front of me. She made my skin crawl. People say she borrowed things and wouldn't give them back. I think she stole things as well. I had a pretty Crown Derby bowl in the Welsh dresser in the sitting room. One day it went missing. When we visited Gloria, there was my bowl. She denied it. I insisted. She burst into tears. Guy said I must be mistaken. Guy and I had a terrible row. I really did hate her. I suppose you really do have to find out who killed her?"

"Poisoning is a nasty, premeditated murder," said Agatha. Unable to bear the smell of the vicar's wife's cigarette smoke, she lit up a cigarette herself. "If someone had just hit her on the head, it wouldn't be so bad."

There came the sound of approaching footsteps. Clarice said urgently, "Here!" and handed her cigarette to Toni before thrusting her lighter back into her brassiere.

The vicar joined them at the table. "Dear me," he said, looking at Toni. "I thought young people knew all about the perils of smoking."

"Never mind that," said Agatha hurriedly. "I am trying to find out all I can about the late Gloria French. You see, the very character of the murdered person can give me a clue to the identity of her murderer."

"The woman was a saint," said the vicar. He flicked a quick warning look at his wife. "She was indefatigable in raising funds for the church. She was a tireless worker."

"Just what I was saying, dear," said Clarice.

"I have heard reports that Gloria was in the habit of borrowing things and not giving them back."

"I think you will find the poor woman had a bad memory."

Agatha realised the vicar had no intention of

speaking ill of the dead. Toni was looking wildly at the long ash at the end of her cigarette, not wanting to follow Agatha's example of flicking ash into the shrubbery. "I'll get you an ashtray," said Clarice, producing one from under a flowerpot.

As Toni stubbed out the cigarette, Agatha asked for directions to Mrs. Ada White's farm and wrote them down.

Agatha did not like visiting farms. They all seemed cursed with muddy yards and savage dogs. But the Whites' farm was trim and clean, a building of mellow Cotswold stone basking in the sunlight.

Ada White came out to meet them. She was a small sturdy woman with rosy cheeks and thick, grey hair. "I was hoping you would call," she said. "Jerry Tarrant told me he had employed you. It's been awful. I know some nasty people have been whispering that it was my wine that poisoned her." Her brown eyes filled with tears. "My elderberry wine has never poisoned anyone. Come into the kitchen."

It was a model kitchen with bunches of aromatic herbs hanging from the ceiling and sunlight shining on large copper pans hung on the walls. A big square wooden table surrounded by Windsor chairs dominated the room. Coffee bubbled in a percolator and there was a smell of fresh baking mingling with the smells of coffee and herbs.

"I have to use the gas stove in this weather," said Ada. "It's too hot for the Aga. Do sit down. Coffee?"

"Please," said Agatha.

Ada bustled about putting mugs, sugar and milk on the table along with a plate of freshly baked scones, a large square of butter and a dish of strawberry jam.

"Do try my scones," she said.

Toni took one and spread it liberally with butter. Agatha could feel her waistband tightening at the very sight of them, but she persuaded herself that one wouldn't hurt. Agatha was always impressed by the sort of women who put the milk in a jug and everything else in its appropriate dish. She always served the milk in its bottle and everything else in whatever container it came in from a shop.

"Now," began Agatha, "who would want to kill Gloria?"

"I think everyone in the village had taken against her," said Ada. "But I can't think of anyone who might be a murderer. We don't have lots of incomers and tourists like the other Cotswold villages."

"Anyone not quite right in the head?" asked Agatha.

"Not a one. In the old days, I believe there were often cases of inbreeding, but everyone has cars these days and the young people even go to the clubs in Birmingham for entertainment. There's nothing to do here and the smoking ban nearly closed down the pub. We all had to start using it to save it."

"That smoking ban has been the death of thousands of pubs," said Agatha bitterly, "but the politically correct won't even breathe that that's the reason. Why couldn't they let pub owners and restaurants just put a smoking or non-smoking sign on their doors and give people a choice the way they do in Barcelona? Now even shops are being ordered to cover up the shelves of cigarettes. Why not cover up the shelves of alcohol? Oh, no, just let the young people go on getting liver damage. Do you know that there are people in their twenties with liver damage? Do you know . . . ?"

"Agatha," interrupted Toni. "What about this murder?"

"Sorry," mumbled Agatha. "What goes into elderberry wine?"

"Just fresh elderberries, sugar, yeast, water and a Campden tablet," said Ada.

"What's a Campden tablet?" asked Agatha.

"Potassium metabisulfite."

"Who would know about rhubarb leaves combined with soda being poisonous?" asked Toni.

"Is that how she died? How awful. I know that

rhubarb leaves are poisonous but I didn't know about adding soda. Most people around here would know about rhubarb leaves."

"Is there anyone who was particularly close to Gloria?" asked Toni. "Did she have any special friend?"

"She spent a lot of time at the vicarage. Maybe she was friendly with the vicar's wife."

Fat chance, thought Agatha.

"Of course, there's old Mrs. Tripp. Gloria spent a long time in her cottage, reading to her."

"Where does she live?" asked Agatha.

"It's the second cottage to the right of the pub. It's called Wonky Wong. She has this rather battered little stone Chinaman on the doorstep."

"Has she always lived there?"

"As long as anyone can remember. She must be nearly ninety."

"Is she a widow?"

"Well, there's the thing. She used to be a cook over at Lady Craton's, just outside Broadway. I think in those days it was a courtesy title. Lady Craton's long dead and her house is an insurance office now."

"But if Mrs. Tripp was in service, she can't have been in the village for long," said Toni.

"The cottage belonged to her parents and she inherited it on their death, quite a long time ago. She let it out while she was in service and then moved into it on her retirement. She certainly knows a lot about the people in the village."

"We'll try her," said Agatha.

"Would you like a bottle of my wine?"

"Yes, please," said Toni quickly, frightened of what her tactless boss might say.

As they drove back towards the village, Agatha said, "You ate three scones, Toni. Don't you ever worry about your figure?"

"No," said Toni cheerfully. "I never seem to put on any weight at all."

Agatha had eaten two and she could feel them nestling somewhere around her waistline.

They knocked at the door of Mrs. Tripp's thatched cottage. The thatch was in good repair. I wonder if Lady Craton left her some money, thought Agatha, knowing from her own bitter experience how much it cost to employ a thatcher.

After quite a wait, Mrs. Tripp answered the door. She was bent over two sticks. Pink scalp was visible through strands of grey hair. Her face was brown and crisscrossed with wrinkles but her eyes looked intelligent.

"You're that detective couple," said Mrs. Tripp. "Bit tarty looking for detectives, ain't you? Come in, come in. Nobody looks like a lady anymore."

They followed her into her cottage parlour. There were four easy chairs covered in bright chintz. Yellow curtains patterned with chrysanthemums fluttered at the open latticed windows. There were some good china ornaments on the mantelpiece. A small table stood at the window covered in silver-framed photographs showing Mrs. Tripp's past life as a cook.

She lowered herself into a chair and Agatha and Toni sat down facing her. "We need your help," said Agatha. "Have you any idea of who might have murdered Gloria?"

"I know who murdered her."

"Tell me," urged Agatha.

"I don't have no one to read to me anymore. If you was to read to me a bit, it'd clear my mind."

"Yes, yes," said Agatha impatiently. "But tell me first."

"Read first, tell afterwards," said the old lady.

"Oh, very well."

Mrs. Tripp took up a book from the side of her chair. It was called *The Duke and the Devil*. The cover portrayed a woman in Regency dress, standing before a burning castle. "Start from page one hundred and two," said Mrs. Tripp.

Agatha crossly handed the book to Toni, who began to read. "Frederica closed her eyes as the duke's hot breath fanned her cheek. 'My stars and garters,' he said. 'You inflame me.' Frederica turned deathly pale. 'Unhand me!' The duke gave a sardonic grin. 'I won you at a game of faro, so you're mine, mine, mine!'"

Snore.

"She's fallen asleep," said Toni.

"Mrs. Tripp," shouted Agatha.

"What!" The old lady woke up and looked about in a dazed way.

"You were about to tell us who murdered Gloria," said Agatha.

"But you haven't read to me."

"Oh, yes we have," said Agatha. "Toni's been reading to you for an hour."

"I could have sworn you only arrived a few minutes ago," said Mrs. Tripp. "Who are you anyway?"

"We're detectives," said Toni gently, "and you really must tell us who murdered Gloria French."

"It was the vicar's wife."

"You're sure?" barked Agatha.

"Saw her with my own eyes going round the back of Gloria's cottage on the morning she was murdered." Her eyelids began to droop and soon she was asleep again.

"Come on, Toni," said Agatha. "Back to the vicarage."

They rang the doorbell but there was no reply. "Maybe she's still in the garden," suggested Toni. They walked round the side of the vicarage, where a high gate stood open. Clarice was sitting in the sunshine, a cigarette in one hand and what looked suspiciously like a glass of elderberry wine in the other.

She started guiltily when she saw them. "Just relaxing," said Clarice. "I find gardening quite exhausting."

"Is that elderberry wine?" demanded Agatha.

"Yes, it is. Was it made by Ada? Yes, it was."

"You were seen going round the back of Gloria's cottage the day she was murdered," said Agatha.

"Oh, do sit down. Yes, I was there."

"Did you tell the police?"

"No, I didn't. It was so awful. I knew she never locked the back door except at night. I suddenly had an impulse to get my Crown Derby bowl back. But when I opened the kitchen door, I heard these noises. I thought Gloria was having sex with someone so I beat it. Oh, God, the poor woman was probably in her death throes and I could have saved her. Please don't tell Guy. Being the vicar's wife, I have to keep up appearances."

"Who did you think she was having sex with?" asked Agatha.

"Henry Bruce. He's by way of being the village's odd job man. He does gardens and repairs things. He's got a colourful reputation and Gloria was a man-eater. You won't tell anyone—please?"

Agatha hesitated. She knew from her friend Mrs. Bloxby that the life of a vicar's wife was not easy. She was expected to do a lot of work around the parish without complaint and keep up appearances at all times.

"I won't say anything," said Agatha. "But it might come out if the forensic team finds anything."

"I don't see how they can," said Clarice. "My fingerprints aren't on file, nor is my DNA."

"Did you see anyone around?" asked Toni.

"No."

"Your fingerprints will be on the door handle. This is a tiny village. The police may get around to taking the fingerprints of everyone in the village."

Clarice clutched her hair. "This is awful! No, it isn't!" She lowered her hands and beamed at Toni. "I wore gloves."

"In this heat!" exclaimed Agatha.

Clarice held out her hands, which were red and rough. "I'm trying to do something about my hands. I covered them in cream and I was wearing white cotton gloves."

"We'll do our best to keep your visit quiet," said Agatha. "We'd better go and see what Henry Bruce has to say for himself. Where does he live?"

"He's got a smallholding just on the left as you go

out of the village. You can't miss it. There's a broken-down tractor in front of his cottage."

Outside the vicarage, Agatha took out her phone and called Patrick. "Any more news?"

"The police have found a couple of footprints on a flowerbed near the back door," said Patrick.

"A woman's footprints?"

"Not unless she wears size tens. The police should be around the place. They're going to check the shoes of every man in the village. There were size-ten footprints on the cellar stairs."

When Agatha rang off, she told Toni the latest news. "That seems to let Clarice out," said Toni. "Her feet are certainly not as big as that."

"Agatha!"

She swung round and found Bill Wong smiling at her. "I gather someone must have employed you," he said. "Who is it?"

"Jerry Tarrant, the head of the parish council," said Agatha.

"Well, we've got officers all over the place. It might be a good idea to leave things just now. Inspector Wilkes is directing operations and he won't like to come across you."

"We're here legitimately," said Agatha. "We'll jump into the shrubbery or something if we see him."

They walked through the village. Policemen could be seen carrying bags of men's shoes and dumping them in the back of police cars. "If they're at Bruce's cottage, we may wait until later," said Agatha. "Gosh, it's hot." She envied Toni, who turned golden brown in the sun whereas all she got was a red face.

They located the cottage with the tractor outside in a small yard. The lazy sound of hens reached their ears.

What would it be like, thought Toni, to live in a little village like this? If one could forget about the murder and the policemen going through the village, and imagine it on a normal day, tucked away as it was from the noise and bustle of the towns, standing in the sun, listening to the soporific clucking of hens, it might have an almost magnetic pull.

But Agatha, striding ahead, shouting, "Anybody home?" shattered the dream.

Agatha had imagined some local village seducer, a sort of Lady Chatterley's lover kind of man. But the figure that emerged from the cottage was a small, slight man with a thick head of black hair, brown eyes and a tanned face. He was wearing a worn blue denim shirt over jeans.

"Mr. Bruce?" asked Agatha.

"That's me. You'll be the detective ladies." He looked Toni over from the top of her blond head to her long tanned legs, displayed to advantage under a short linen skirt. He smiled at her. "You can interrogate me any time. What's your name?"

"Agatha Raisin," said Agatha crossly, interposing herself between Toni and Henry.

"And who's the pretty one, then?"

"My assistant, Toni Gilmour. Is there anywhere we can talk?"

"Come inside."

They followed him into the coolness of a stone-flagged kitchen. "Sit down," he said. Agatha and Toni sat on plastic chairs at a plastic table. Toni looked around. The kitchen appliances were ancient. She wondered if he collected people's broken-down fridges and cookers and repaired them. The cooker was of chipped green enamel and looked as if it dated from the forties. There was also a washing machine with a mangle.

"Drink?" he offered, opening an old fridge. It seemed to be full of nothing but cans of beer.

"No, thanks," said Agatha.

He helped himself to a beer, sat down at the table and smiled lazily at Toni. "Fire away."

"Were you having an affair with Gloria French?" asked Agatha.

"She lived in hope, that one," he said. "But why would I be interested in an old bird like that when there are gorgeous girls around?"

"I haven't seen any gorgeous girls in this village," said Agatha.

"I go up to Birmingham occasionally. Clubbing."

Agatha estimated Henry was in his forties. "Aren't you a bit old to go clubbing?"

"Never too old, and it would amaze you to see how willing those girls are."

"So what can you tell me about Gloria?" said Agatha.

"Don't you let your pretty sidekick open her mouth?" Agatha glared at him.

"Oh, well, let's see. Gloria. She wanted me to unblock her sink. I did that. But when I tried to charge her, she pressed up against me and said she could pay in other ways. I ran. She called on me several times after that before she gave up. She was a right harpy."

"Have the police taken your shoes?" asked Toni.

"Came here just before you."

"What size shoe do you take?" asked Agatha.

"Size nine."

"Have you any idea who might have murdered her?" asked Agatha.

He shook his head. "She did annoy a lot of people by taking things and not giving them back."

"Was there ever anything valuable?"

"Not that I heard. Oh, yes. There was one thing. Lady Framington."

"Who's she?"

"Our lady of the manor, that's what. Gloria had organised a dance in the village hall. She borrowed a string of real pearls from Samantha Framington and she had a hell of a job getting them back. If they hadn't been listed on her insurance, I think Gloria would have hung on to them."

"But," said Toni, "if Gloria had such a reputation, why did someone like Mrs. Framington lend her valuable pearls?"

"That was shortly after Gloria moved into the village. Everyone thought she was great. She seemed to do such a lot of good work."

"Where did Gloria come from?"

"London, I think."

"Where is the manor?"

"Big square house at the other end of the village from here."

The trouble with wearing a sun hat, thought Agatha, as they plodded their way along to the manor house, was that it upset one's hairdo. But as the sun beat down on her head, she reluctantly decided she would need to stop at her car and get an old straw one out of the back.

"We'll take the car," she said.

"Why? We're nearly there," said Toni.

"Because the damn place might have a drive and I'm hot and tired."

Agatha drove in through the open gates of the manor. Lawns stretched on either side. There didn't seem to be a bit of shade. Toni was glad to get back out into the sunshine because Agatha had blasted the air-conditioning so high that she had goose bumps on her arms.

The manor house was a square Georgian building with a portico. It looked well kept and prosperous. Agatha rang a polished brass bell set into the stonework at the side of the door. They waited.

The door was opened by a small man wearing a green baize apron.

"Lady Framington?" asked Agatha.

"No, I'm the butler, or maid of all work. I've been polishing the silver. If you're selling anything, shove off."

"My name is Agatha Raisin," said Agatha haughtily. "Here is my card. I wish to speak to Lady Framington."

"Whether she'll want to speak to you is another matter." The butler slammed the door in their faces.

Toni giggled. "Honestly. Talk about the servant problem."

But deep down in Agatha's psyche lay the memory of her upbringing in a Birmingham slum and she felt outraged.

The door opened again. "She'll see you," said the butler. "Follow me."

Agatha followed his small figure, resisting a sudden urge to kick him in the backside. He led them out onto a terrace at the back of the house. Lady Framington was sitting at a table reading a glossy magazine.

She looked up and saw Agatha. "Oh, you're that detective woman. Sit down. Fred, bring tea."

"Can't. I'm polishing the silver."

"Just do it, you horrible little toad."

Fred went off, grumbling under his breath.

"Is he always like that?" asked Agatha.

"Yes, but he's got arthritis and it makes him grumpy. One must make allowances."

She had a "county" voice and a manner reminiscent of Maggie Smith playing the part of the dowager in *Downton Abbey*. She had large hands and feet and a slim flat-chested figure dressed in a faded cotton shirt-waister. A large collagen-enhanced mouth dominated her face. Her hair was iron grey and cropped short.

"I am investigating the death of Gloria French," said Agatha. There was no shade on the terrace and a smooth lawn stretched out in front. No flowers or bushes.

"So I heard. Quite exciting. Gloria was a pill."

"I hear you had some trouble getting a necklace back."

"That damn woman tried to steal it. At first, she seemed like God's gift, doing good works all over the place. But incomers often go on like that and then they settle down. She backed down fast when I said I had proof of ownership and I would take her to court. Any idea who did it so I can shake the murderer's hand?"

"Not yet," said Agatha. "Have you any idea who might have wanted to kill her?"

Lady Framington picked up a brass bell on the table and rang it energetically. The butler appeared through the French windows. "Where's the bloody tea, Fred?"

"Just bloody coming."

The butler retreated. "Ever watch Poirot?" asked Lady Framington.

"Yes," said Agatha.

"I always know whodunit. I bet I can find out who this murderer is. Whether I would tell you is another matter. Here's the tea at last."

There were no biscuits or cakes. Just a brown china pot of tea, milk and sugar and three mugs.

"Help yourself," said Lady Framington.

"Lady Framington . . ."

"Sam, please."

"Well, Sam," said Agatha, "if you go detecting and get too close, the murderer might want to remove you."

Sam gave a great braying laugh. "I can take care of myself. Drink up."

The tea was awful: dark brown and stewed, but Sam drank hers with relish. "Fred does make a good cup of tea."

"Isn't that someone at the bottom of your garden?" cried Agatha.

"What? Where?"

Agatha quickly poured her tea under the table.

"I can't see anything," said Sam.

"Must have been mistaken. If you think of anyone, please let me know," said Agatha. "Come along, Toni."

When Agatha and Toni had gone, Sam rang the bell. "What now?" asked Fred, answering its summons.

"Clear the table."

"Look at that!" said Fred, pointing to a damp patch under the chair where Agatha had been sitting. "She pissed herself. Dirty old cow."

Back in her car, Agatha said, "Let's go back to the Green Man."

"Why?" asked Toni.

"They've got rooms. I think I should book one and

move in tomorrow. You handle the office while I'm away. Simon can join me."

The following day, Simon and Toni went out for lunch. "I don't want to go," said Simon. "I don't want to be stuck in some village in this heat."

"It is a murder enquiry," said Toni.

"The thought of Agatha's company, staying at a pub without air-conditioning, depresses me no end. Got a boyfriend, Toni?"

"Yes," said Toni, "and don't say a word to Agatha. You know she always interferes."

"Who is he?"

"Mind your own business."

"So no hope for me?"

"Cut it out, Simon."

Simon laughed to cover up the yearning he always felt in Toni's company. He was small in stature with a jester's mobile face and a thick thatch of black hair. He wondered who Toni's new beau was and whether he was tall and handsome.

"And what about Agatha?" asked Simon. "Fallen in love again?"

"No, our boss is obsession free for once in her life, and, believe me, there's no one in Piddlebury to attract her."

Later that day, Agatha was shown up to a low-raftered room in the pub. At least a tree outside the window provided some shade. She turned to the landlord, Moses Green. "Where's the bathroom?"

"Turn left as you go out of your room. It's at the end of the corridor."

After he had left, Agatha unpacked. Then picking up her sponge bag and towel, she decided to have a wash because she felt hot and sticky. But the bathroom door was locked.

"Anyone in there?" called Agatha.

"Won't be a minute," called a masculine voice.

Agatha waited patiently. Then the door opened and a tall man stood there. He was naked apart from a towel wrapped round his waist. His bare chest was hairless, white and muscled. Agatha felt a small surge of lust. Welcome back, she said mentally to her hormones. I thought you had died.

He held out a hand. "I'm Brian Summer."

"Agatha Raisin," said Agatha, feeling an electric tingle going up her arm. He had a thick shock of white hair, intelligent grey eyes and an interesting face. Agatha estimated that he was the same age as she was herself.

"Are you on holiday?" asked Agatha.

"Yes. I need a bit of relaxation. Now, if you'll excuse me?"

I didn't get his name, thought Agatha. He's very attractive. Snakes and bastards! My make-up must have melted.

There was no shower, only a deep bath standing on claw feet, a relic of the Edwardian era. It seemed to take ages to run.

At last Agatha was bathed, made up and dressed in a short white linen skirt, red linen blouse and very high heels. Simon had the room next door. She shouted to him that she would be in the pub garden.

She made her way to the bar where the landlord was polishing glasses. "I met your other visitor," said Agatha.

"Ah, that would be Mr. Summer."

"Does he usually holiday here?"

"First time. He says he's a chemistry teacher."

That's a non-starter, thought Agatha gloomily. What I know of chemistry couldn't even fill the back of a postage stamp. She collected a gin and tonic and made her way out into the garden.

Brian was sitting at a table, reading. He did not look up as Agatha made her entrance. She decided it would be too pushy to go and join him.

Simon appeared carrying a glass of lager. "Oh, look, Agatha," he said. "One big glass ashtray. You can smoke yourself silly."

But Agatha was frightened her new quarry might be anti-smoking. "I've given up," she said crossly, fighting down a longing to light up.

And then her heart began to beat, because Brian Summer rose and came to their table. "Mind if I join you?" he asked.

"Oh, please do. This is Simon Black, one of my detectives."

"It's all over the village that you're here to solve the murder," said Brian. He was wearing a grey shirt and grey trousers.

"How far have you got?" asked Brian.

Agatha told him about her interviews. When she had finished, he asked, "And now what do you do?"

"Just keep asking," said Agatha. "Believe me, someone in this village knows something."

"I've never tasted elderberry wine," said Brian. "What's it like?"

"You can try some now if you like. Simon, I've got a bottle in the car. Bring it in and get Moses to give you three glasses. The car's not locked."

When Simon had gone, Agatha rested her chin on her hands and smiled at Brian in what she hoped was a winsome way. "Tell me all about yourself."

"There's nothing to tell," he said. "I am simply here for a quiet holiday."

"Won't your family miss you?"

"I haven't got a family."

Simon came rushing back. Agatha scowled at him. "The bottle's gone," said Simon. "Are you sure it was there?"

"I haven't touched it since Ada White gave it to me," said Agatha. "It was still there when we arrived at this pub."

"Someone must have pinched it," said Simon. "Shall I tell the police?"

"They're not going to bother about a bottle of wine," said Agatha. "Not with a murder case to solve. Brian, you were just telling me about yourself."

He rose abruptly. "I've got to go. Excuse me."

Agatha sadly watched his tall figure hurrying away.

Later that night, a full moon rose over the village. Up in the woods, full-time layabout and part-time poacher Craig Upton took the bottle of elderberry wine he had thieved from Agatha's car from one of the capacious pockets in his smelly coat, which he wore despite the warmth of the night. He settled his back against the trunk of a large oak tree and unscrewed the top. Craig's arthritis had been getting worse lately. He was in his eighties and dreaded the day when he would have to give up his country life and move into some nursing home. He fished a tumbler out of another pocket. He prided himself on never drinking anything straight from the bottle. He filled the glass and held it up. The liquid glinted black in the moonlight. He liked to drink the first glass of any alcohol straight down and then drink the rest in more modest gulps.

"Here's health," he said. He poured the liquid down his throat.

Chapter Three

Moses Green woke early and took his Labrador dog, Jess, for a walk in the woods. He liked to get away from the pub and into the cool shade of the trees. Jess ran ahead of him, the flickering sunlight shining down through the leaves glinting on her glossy black coat. She had run a good bit ahead of Moses when he heard her let out a great howl. Fearing she had got caught in some trap, Moses raced towards the sound of that horrible howl.

He stopped short and looked at the dreadful scene that met his eyes. Craig Upton lay twisted up at the foot of an oak tree, his eyes staring upwards. His clothes were covered in foul-smelling vomit. Flies buzzed around him. Moses put his dog on the leash and pulled her back and tied the leash to a branch. He felt for a pulse but found none. He saw the bottle of elderberry wine lying beside the body.

He unhitched Jess's leash from the branch and began to run.

Agatha awoke to the sound of wailing sirens. She scrambled into her clothes and then banged on Simon's door, shouting, "Something's happened. I'm going outside."

People were appearing outside their cottages, some still in their nightwear. Agatha saw Peter Suncliff and went to join him. "What's going on?"

"Something up in the woods."

"Where?"

"Up there. Behind the pub."

Agatha set off at a run. She saw the white suits of a forensic team up ahead as she entered the woods and followed them. An area around an oak tree had been taped off and a tent erected.

Bill Wong was standing talking to another detective. "Bill!" shouted Agatha. "What's happened?"

He came to join her. "Get out of here, Agatha.

Wilkes is on his way and he'll be furious if he finds you poking around."

"But what's going on?"

"Another case of poisoning and it looks like elderberry wine."

Agatha suddenly looked stricken. "Bill, I had a bottle of elderberry wine in my car. Someone pinched it yesterday evening. Mrs. White gave it to me the day before yesterday."

"Here comes Inspector Wilkes," said Bill. "You'd better tell him about this."

"But who's dead?"

"Some local poacher."

"What the hell is she doing here?" demanded Wilkes. Bill told him.

"There's a mobile police unit just arrived," said Wilkes. "I want you to go down there, Mrs. Raisin, and wait until I can take your statement."

On the road back, Agatha met Simon and told him what had happened. "Don't you see?" she exclaimed. "Someone was trying to poison me. We could all have been poisoned—you, me and Brian. I've got to go to the mobile police unit and wait for Wilkes."

They walked together down into the village. It was another glorious day: a day for village fetes, not for murder.

"I suppose the press will be all over this," said Agatha.

"The police have already blocked off entrances to the village to keep them out," said Simon. "Some have arrived. Lots more will probably come later."

They walked into the mobile police unit, which was parked in front of the church.

There were two policemen and Detective Sergeant Alice Peterson. "Why, Mrs. Raisin," said Alice. "Got news for me?"

Agatha sat down opposite her. "I've got to make a statement to Wilkes."

"I'll wait outside," said Simon. "It's hot as hell in here."

Agatha told Alice about the theft of the wine from her car. "So," said Alice when she had finished, "the poisoned wine may have been meant for you."

Agatha stared at her. Although she had told Bill that might be the case, the full horror of it struck her.

Despite the heat in the mobile unit, she felt suddenly cold.

A policeman came in carrying an electric fan, which he plugged in. It blew the hot air around and sent papers fluttering on desks.

Agatha sat slowly down on a hard plastic chair. It seemed ages before Wilkes arrived, but glancing at her watch, Agatha realised she had only been waiting ten minutes.

Wilkes pulled a chair forward and sat down opposite Agatha, his thin grey face a mask of disapproval. Why, he wondered, were most of his cases cluttered up by this bossy woman getting underfoot?

"Now, Mrs. Raisin," he began, "tell me about this bottle of elderberry wine."

"Mrs. Ada White gave me a bottle. I was in the pub last night with Simon Black and Brian Summer, a guest staying at the pub. He said he had never tasted elderberry wine before. I remembered the bottle Mrs. White had given me and sent Simon out to get it. He came back and said it had gone."

"Had you locked your car?"

"No."

"Forget?"

"I didn't think it mattered in a village like this."

"With a murderer around, everything matters, Mrs. Raisin. We will check the bottle for fingerprints. We have yours on record. But as Mrs. White seems to be an upstanding member of the community, we must assume that someone substituted that bottle for another. Wong has gone to see her. Now, Mrs. Raisin, you are adding to our difficulties. It would be safer for you to leave the village."

"I have been employed to find out who murdered Gloria French," said Agatha, "and I intend to go on searching."

Wilkes questioned her about who she had interviewed, making her go over it again and again. When she had finished, he said, "Don't do anything to interfere in our enquiries or I'll have you locked up for obstructing the police. Now, wait until your statement is ready, sign it and get out of my sight! But first, tell Simon Black to get in here."

Agatha went out into the heat of the day and told Simon that Wilkes wanted to see him. She stood outside, irresolute, looking at the policemen going door to door.

Somewhere in this picture-postcard village was a murderer. Agatha trailed back to the pub. She wanted a cool drink under a tree in the garden.

Agatha paused at the entrance to the pub garden. Seated under the shade of a cypress tree was Charles Fraith.

"What are you doing here?" demanded Agatha, walking up to him. Her voice was sharp because she did not want to betray how very glad she was to see him. He smiled up at her lazily. "Came to see how you were getting on. Sit down and tell me what's been happening."

Agatha sat down opposite him. "How did you get

into the village? The police are stopping anyone getting in."

"I came last night. Late. You'd gone to bed by that time."

Agatha wondered how it was that Charles never seemed to feel the heat. He was dressed in a pale blue cotton shirt, open at the neck, and darker blue chinos. His fair hair was as impeccably barbered as ever and his neat catlike features only portrayed amusement.

I have slept with this man, thought Agatha, and yet, not by one flicker does he ever betray any intimacy. We go on like a couple of old bachelors. Moses came out and asked her what she would like to drink. Agatha ordered a gin and tonic, adding, "Do make sure this gentleman pays for it."

"That was rude," commented Charles.

"I just couldn't bear to hear you say you'd forgotten your wallet one more time. Anyway, here's the latest."

Agatha told him about the dead poacher and the fact that the poisoned wine might have been meant for her.

"Don't you think it might be a good idea to leave this village alone until things settle down?" suggested Charles. "A dead detective isn't much use."

Agatha accepted her drink from Moses and said

with a sigh, "Whoever it is could just as well come after me in Mircester as here."

"So what's your next move?"

"I'll finish my drink and then I'll try to see Jerry Tarrant. He's the head of the parish council who employed me. He might have some ideas. By the way, do you know the lady of the manor, Sam Framington?"

"Don't think so."

"She wants to detect and might be putting herself at risk."

"Maybe we'll call on her after Jerry," said Charles. "Ready?"

"Wait for me a moment. I've got to repair my make-up."

"Who is he?"

"Don't be silly, Charles. I won't be long."

When Agatha returned to the pub garden, she saw to her dismay that Charles was deep in conversation with Brian Summer. Charles grinned when he saw her, taking in Agatha in all her glory of fresh make-up, green linen blouse, and green linen shorts, showing her excellent legs. At least she hasn't put high heels on, thought Charles.

"Hullo, Brian," said Agatha brightly. She was about

to sit down but Charles stood up and said firmly, "We'd better go."

"No rush," said Agatha. "I could do with another drink."

"Better keep your brains sharp," said Charles. "Come along."

"See you later," said Agatha hopefully to Brian.

"Really, Aggie," said Charles as they made their way out of the pub. "You never give up."

"I find him interesting," said Agatha haughtily. "Let's take my car."

"Where does Jerry live?"

Agatha consulted her notes. "The other side of the church. His house is called Stoneways."

"So it's just along there. We can walk."

"Not while I've got air-conditioning in the car."

Unlike the other houses, Stoneways was set back from the road with a small driveway. It was a Georgian house of mellow stone covered in ivy.

"It's a wonder he lets that ivy stay," said Charles. "I'd cut it down. It's nearly covering all the windows."

They got out of the car. Agatha rang the bell. While they waited, Charles said, "We should really be going to see Ada White."

"No use at the moment," said Agatha. "The police are probably all over her place."

The door opened and Jerry, looking flustered, said, "Oh, do come in. I thought it might be the police back again. I am so tired of answering questions."

"This is Charles Fraith," said Agatha.

"Another of your detectives?"

"Yes," said Charles quickly.

They followed him into a gloomy study, which had a subterranean air caused by the green leaves of the ivy outside, practically blocking the window.

The room was as neat as its owner, with bookshelves along one wall, the books arranged by colour rather than alphabet. Jerry sat down behind an antique desk, ornamented only by an equally antique silver inkstand. Behind him, on the wall, was a badly executed portrait of himself in oils. A large Regency mirror hung over the fireplace. In a display cabinet in one corner were glowing pieces of china: figurines and plates.

"This latest news is terrible," said Jerry. "Who would want to poison that old poacher?"

"He took the wine from my car, or that's the way it looks," said Agatha. "The police think the poison might have been meant for me."

"This is terrible!" cried Jerry. "You must stop whoever it is."

"I'll do my best," said Agatha, "but it is difficult

with the police all over the village. Now, let's discuss Gloria. As far as I know, she simply borrowed things and never gave them back."

"She also stole things."

"You didn't tell me that."

"I'm telling you now. While we thought she was just a harmless do-gooder, I invited her to a dinner party. On the following day, I discovered a little Meissen shepherd and shepherdess were missing from that cabinet over there. I didn't want to call the police and cause a scandal before I had asked around. Clarice, the vicar's wife, was at the dinner party. She shocked me by suggesting that Gloria might have taken them. I thought she was jealous because Gloria had been flirting like mad with the vicar. We don't lock our doors in this village—or we didn't used to—so I waited until I saw her go off for one of her long confabs with the vicar over the church restoration and let myself into her cottage. I could hardly believe my eyes. There were my china ornaments on her mantelpiece. I simply took them back."

"So what did she say when you told her?" asked Charles.

Jerry flushed slightly. "Truth to tell, I hadn't the courage. She was very bossy and she frightened me. When I met her again, she went on as if nothing had happened. I feel so ashamed now. If I had reported the loss to the police and she had been found guilty, people would have stopped lending her things and they would have watched their belongings. And she had got herself elected to the parish council. But there was worse to come."

"Go on," urged Agatha.

"There was a party in the church hall to celebrate the repair of the church roof. Of course, it was all to congratulate Gloria on her work. The vicar made a moving speech and his wife looked as if she didn't know whether to throttle him or Gloria. Well, Gloria drank a lot.

"I had just got home and was about to open my door when I heard her calling me. She came right up to me, stinking of scent. 'Let's have a bit of fun, Jerry,' she said, and she pressed herself up against me."

"And what happened then?" asked Charles.

"I thrust her away and screamed for help. She turned round and tottered off."

"Her murder may not have anything to do with her taking things," said Agatha. "If she was that hot, maybe she was having an affair with someone—or in her case, anyone. Can you think of anyone?"

"It can't be our vicar, Guy Enderbury."

"Why?" asked Agatha.

"His wife would gouge her eyes out. I think Clarice was the very first to get wise to her. There is Peter

Suncliff. She really did chase after him. I find middle-aged women who pursue men disgusting!"

"I couldn't agree more," said Charles, flicking an amused look at Agatha.

"But poison is supposed to be a woman's choice of weapon," said Agatha.

"Usually, I believe," said Jerry. "But if someone wanted her dead by slipping a bottle of poisoned wine among the others she had, then they would have an alibi for the time of death. And how would anyone know that she would drink that particular bottle on that particular day and so be on hand to remove the evidence? And what about substituting the wine in your car for the poisoned one?"

"It would only take a moment," said Agatha. "So many of the villagers seem to use the pub and like a fool I left my car unlocked. What about Samantha Framington? She leant Gloria her pearls and had to fight to get them back. If only the damn woman had reported that to the police."

"Just like me," said Jerry gloomily.

"What now?" asked Charles. Agatha's phone rang. She turned away to answer the call, walking a bit away from him. He could hear from the cooing note in Agatha's usually robust voice that something was pleasing her. When she rang off and joined him, she said excitedly, "That was Cambridge TV. They want to do an interview with me tomorrow on their morning show. Of course, they're not in Cambridge. That's the name of the owner. Have you seen the show? It's called *Good Morning, Britain*."

"No, but I've read the reviews. It's supposed to be pretty awful."

"I can kill two birds with one stone. I'll get Patrick to dig up Gloria's former address in London and interview some of her old neighbours. Are you coming with me?"

Charles grinned. "Wouldn't miss it for worlds. What about young Simon?"

"I think I'll send him back to the office until things quieten down here. I don't want to come back and find him poisoned."

The studios of *Good Morning, Britain* were situated in Canary Wharf. Agatha and Charles had to go through many irritating security checks by guards in the vast car park underneath the building.

At last Agatha was seated, getting her make-up done. A man rushed into the room. "I'm the producer, Tristram Guise," he said. "I'm afraid there's been a bit of a cock-up. Before your interview, we'd scheduled an Indian cooking lesson, but the chef refused to come."

"Why?" demanded Agatha.

"The cheapskate wanted us to pay his taxi fare to the studio."

"Was he coming from Birmingham?" Birmingham is the home of the best curries.

"No, Fulham."

"Wouldn't it have been a good idea just to pay his fare?" asked Agatha.

"Well, the damage is done. The thing is, we've rented all this kitchen equipment and we've got to cover the cost. Can you cook up a curry?"

"Only if it comes in a plastic container and I can put it in the microwave," said Agatha.

"Look, you've got to cook something. It's too late to get anyone else. What about an omelette?"

"I suppose I can do that."

"Robin, our researcher, will help you. Right, let's get to it. Oh, here's someone to mike you up. Just give the viewers a speech about simple dishes being the best and yaddy-ya."

Agatha was not about to tell anyone that she had never cooked an omelette in her life before, but she had watched Mrs. Bloxby doing it. What could go wrong?

She was escorted along to the studio, where she was wrapped in a striped apron and told to stand behind a stove. Robin, a small dark-haired girl, smiled at her.

"Isn't there a smell of gas?" asked Agatha.

"We fixed up a butane gas canister. It's fine. Here we go. You've got the frying pan, butter and a box of eggs."

The lights went down in the studio. The presenter, a willowy blonde, sat on a red sofa, practising her smile. The floor manager began the countdown. Agatha suddenly experienced a feeling of pure panic.

The lights went up. "We are honoured to have with us, this morning, our favourite private eye, Agatha Raisin," said the presenter. "But as she's also by way of being a village lady, she's first going to show you lucky viewers how to cook an omelette. Sorry we couldn't bring your Aga, Agatha. That's what you village dames use. Over to you, Agatha."

Agatha cleared her throat. "First, you melt some butter in a frying pan. That's if you've switched on the gas. Is the gas switched on?"

"Sorry," said Robin, turning a knob.

"And we wait for it to melt while we beat up the eggs." Agatha felt her confidence growing. She whipped up four eggs in a bowl with a fork, added salt and put the mixture in the pan. "Now, while we wait for it to cook," she said cheerfully, "let me tell you about my latest case. What?"

"The gas's very high," whispered Robin. "You'd better flip the omelette before it scorches."

"Right!" All Agatha's nervousness came rushing back. She seized a spatula, put it under the omelette and gave it a hearty toss. It went straight up and stuck on the studio ceiling.

"Cut," said the producer. "Go to the ads. Robin, you do the omelette quickly."

"I'll try," said Robin, "but the gas pressure's dying. Are you sure there isn't a leak?"

"Get on with it!"

Agatha felt suddenly dizzy. She walked over to the presenter. "Could we just get on with the interview?"

There came a crash behind her as Robin slumped to the floor.

"Get a doctor," said the presenter.

"I think she's gassed," said Agatha. "I'm sure there's a leak."

"Just get back there," shouted the producer as two men carried Robin out. "Wind it up as if nothing had happened. Say something about simple country cooking being the best. A studio hand has disconnected the gas cylinder. You'll be all right."

Agatha reluctantly took her place behind the stove.

"And that, viewers, is how you make an omelette. I always think that . . ."

But that was as far as Agatha got. The omelette detached itself from the ceiling and landed on her head.

Charles, watching the whole scene on the monitor in the greenroom, could hardly stop laughing.

A flustered-looking man put his head round the door. "Mrs. Raisin is asking for you. She wants to leave."

"Where is she?"

"Getting her hair washed."

"Well, she won't need me to help her with that. What's happening about her interview? Who's that warbling on the screen?"

"We'd got this Gaelic singer who was supposed to do a number to end the show. Now, she's got the whole show."

Charles settled back to wait. Agatha eventually joined him.

"How's that girl doing who passed out?"

"Recovering in the sickbay demanding a lawyer. Oh, let's get out of here, Charles. I feel so humiliated."

"Agatha, it was the funniest thing you've ever seen. The press will be after you."

"Let them try. I don't want any more publicity. I just want away from this Mickey Mouse studio."

"Cheer up. They did a nice job with your hair."

Once they were driving away from Canary Wharf, Agatha said, "Patrick has texted me with Gloria's former address. It's a mews house, Southern Mews, off the Gloucester Road. Let's just hope I can find a parking place."

Agatha felt the gods had decided at last to be merciful as she slid her car into a parking place on the Gloucester Road near the entrance to the mews.

"She lived at number four," said Agatha. "Let's start at number five."

They walked into the cobbled mews, a pretty lane of whitewashed houses, some decorated with hanging baskets of flowers.

Agatha rang the bell of number five. A tall grey-haired woman answered the door. She looked at Agatha in surprise and then burst out laughing. Then she called over her shoulder, "Come here, Paul. It's that woman from the telly—you know, the one with the omelette on her head."

Agatha angrily made to turn away but Charles seized her arm in a firm grip. Paul joined the woman at the door and grinned at Agatha. "You were a hoot," he said.

"We're actually investigating the murder of Gloria French," said Charles quickly. "She used to live next door to you, didn't she?"

"You'd better come in. I'm Debbie and this is Paul."

"I'm Charles and this, as you know, is the famous Agatha Raisin," said Charles, giving Agatha a little push in the back as she seemed reluctant to go into the mews house. As mews houses had once been for coaches with accommodation for the coachman abovestairs and faced north, the living room was dark. It was furnished with leather-and-chrome chairs and violent abstract paintings swearing down from white-painted walls. Like his wife, Paul was tall with grey hair. He urged them to sit down while he and his wife folded themselves into low chairs.

"Please do not talk about that television show," said Agatha. "We really need to know all we can about Gloria. What was she like?"

"Pushy, common and grasping," said Debbie. "We're a quiet lot in this mews. The walls are thin. Gloria made a pass at Paul and was rejected. But she stopped me one morning and said, 'Has Paul asked for a divorce yet?' I asked her what she was talking about and she said, 'Oh, you poor deluded woman,' and just walked away.

"Fact is, I thought Paul was having it off with that

new blond secretary of his and we had a terrible row. Now, Gloria had a best friend, Carrie James, at number ten. But Carrie went off her and told us that on the evening we were having that row, Gloria had a tumbler pressed to the wall, listening to as much as she could. She was a nasty troublemaker and I hope she died a horrible death. When's the funeral? I've a good mind to send a wreath of rhubarb leaves."

"Do you happen to know if any of your neighbours ever visited her in that village she moved to?" asked Charles.

"I think Carrie went there. She said Gloria had something of hers she wanted back."

"We'd better see Carrie," said Agatha.

As they emerged into the mews, a small boy ran up to Agatha waving an autograph book. "May I have your autograph?"

"Sure." Agatha signed a page with a flourish and smiled indulgently at the little boy. "Want to be a detective when you grow up?"

"No, I want to be on telly. You were ace. My mum says the whole thing was staged, but it was funny all the same."

"Run along, *dear*," said Agatha through gritted teeth.

"Cheer up, Aggie," said Charles. "If people think

the whole thing was staged for a laugh, they'll forget about it pretty quickly. Here's number ten. Let's hope she's at home."

When what turned out to be Carrie James opened the door to them, Agatha's first impression of the woman was that she looked like a lizard. It was her eyes, which were long-shaped and bright green under heavy lids. She had straight fair hair and was wearing a Chinese kimono over a nightdress.

Agatha introduced herself and Charles and explained they wanted to talk to her about Gloria.

"I can't help you," said Carrie. Her voice was low and husky. "Horrible woman."

"May we come in?" asked Agatha.

"No."

"You visited her in Piddlebury. Why?"

"Went down to get my wineglasses back."

"And did you get them?"

"Oh, yes."

"How?"

"What do you mean 'how'?"

"Well," said Agatha, striving for patience, "I gather she had a way of holding on to things she had borrowed."

"I threatened to sue her."

"Did you kill her?"

"Get off my doorstep or I'll kill you." Carrie slammed the door in their faces.

They patiently worked their way along the mews, asking people who were at home about Gloria.

All the replies were unfavourable and terse.

Number eight: "Common as muck."

Number seven: "Horrible grasping creature."

Number two: "I'm glad she's dead. Push off."

"I don't think we should hang around waiting for the rest to come home," said Charles. "Don't you feel that our murderer is in Piddlebury?"

"You're probably right," said Agatha. "I thought neighbours in London didn't know each other but Gloria seems to have riled up everyone here."

"Let's have something to eat," said Charles. "There's a restaurant over there."

When they were eating sandwiches and drinking coffee, Agatha said, "I wonder if she had a hold over someone in the village. Look at the way she left the vicarage dinner party to thieve a bit of china. What if she found love letters, something like that, in someone's house. I think Gloria was the sort who would enjoy a bit of blackmail."

"Could be. But if she was holding on to anything

incriminating, the police would have found it when they searched the house."

Agatha phoned Patrick. "You've got a list of people in that village. You'll find it on my computer. See if anyone has a criminal record. Oh, and there's a visitor at the inn, a chemistry teacher, Brian Summer. See what you can get on him."

"Fancy him, do you?" asked Charles.

"What are you talking about?"

"This fellow, Brian Summer. You don't really suspect him. You just want some leverage there."

"Nonsense. In my book, everyone's a suspect. Oh, do shut up and let me eat in peace."

They were just finishing their meal when Agatha's phone rang. It was Patrick. "Brian Summer was involved in a case a few months ago," he said. "He dropped into a party some of his pupils were having to celebrate the end of term before the Easter holidays. A sixteen-year-old girl was found dead in one of the bedrooms in the morning. It was found at the autopsy that she had drunk GBL."

"What's that?"

"It's a substance called gamma-butyrolactone. Get it in paint stripper or stuff for cleaning alloy wheels. Known on the street as 'coma in a bottle.' I think it was banned last December but before that anyone could order it off the Internet. It's tasteless and can be mixed, say, in orange juice. It gives a high like ecstasy, and it's very cheap. A small bottle costs around twenty-three pounds and contains enough for fifty shots. Because traces of it disappear after twelve hours, it may be responsible for a lot of unexplained deaths. It can be used as a date rape drug. Too much causes death."

"And so what happened to Brian Summer?"

"When they didn't know what had killed her and suspected poisoning, and with him being a chemistry teacher, he was pulled in for questioning. Nearly cost him his job. Then one of the boys told the police that they had brought along a bottle of this GBL. They were mixing it with fruit juice. But it's easier to overdose on GBL than heroin. Get the concentration even slightly wrong and you can end up unconscious or dead."

"Surely they must have had something more on him than the fact he was a chemistry teacher?"

"He was the only adult there. It was a bit of a drunken rave, so what was a teacher doing at such a party?"

"And what was his explanation?"

"Don't know. Seems he is popular, particularly with the girls. He had promised to drop in. Actually, it turned out he was only there ten minutes."

When Agatha rang off, she told Charles the latest news. He gave her a mocking look. "You're too old for him, I think. Maybe he fancies the young ones."

"Nonsense," said Agatha. "He did not strike me as being like that at all."

"But . . ."

"Drop it!" snarled Agatha.

"Oh, well, back to the village of the damned."

As they sat in the pub garden that evening, Agatha hoping that Brian would turn up, and avoiding the amused looks of the villagers who appeared to have seen, or heard about, her disaster in the studio kitchen, Charles asked, "Who's the Framington female married to? You didn't say anything about him."

"If there was one, I didn't see him," said Agatha. "Let's go and see her. I've a feeling she knows something."

"What! Before dinner?"

"Won't take long."

On the road out, Agatha asked Moses about Sam's husband.

"That would be Lord Cyril Framington. Died last year."

"What of?"

"A stroke."

"Old title?"

"No, a Labour peer. Died in the House of Lords, he did."

78

"Where have all the press gone?"

"The police are keeping them out of the village," said Moses. "Pity. Great drinkers, the press."

Outside the pub, they met Brian Summer. Agatha hailed him. "Have a drink with us later?"

Brian smiled. "Kind of you but I think I'll have an early night."

"Exit first murderer," whispered Charles as they walked off.

"Oh, do shut up," snapped Agatha, "and if you and Samantha know people in common, forget it. I don't want to sit there while you yap on about people I've never heard of. It's still so hot. I wish we had taken my car."

"Can't be far," said Charles. "This is one tiny village."

"We're here," said Agatha.

They walked up the drive and rang the bell. Fred answered the door. "Oh, it's you," he said.

"Yes, it is indeed," said Agatha. "So hop to it."

"Cheeky!" Fred slammed the door on them.

"I do so hate characters," said Charles. "Will he return?"

"Oh, sure, just playing one of his nasty little power games."

The door opened again and Fred jerked his head. They followed him in. He flung open a door and said, "She's back."

Sam rose to her feet. "Who is this with you?"

"Charles Fraith," said Agatha, who was determined not to use Charles's title in case it unleashed a flood of the "Do you know the Wilkinson-Sword-Blades? How is old Buffy?" type of reminiscence in which she could have no part.

They found themselves in a pleasant sitting room with long French windows overlooking the garden at the back.

The furnishings were, Charles decided, of a style he damned as country-house-to-order. Everything looked as if it had been delivered from the shop all on the same day. Family portraits on the walls were actually photographs treated to look like oil paintings. The furniture was fake Louis XV. Maybe they spent all their money contributing to the Labour Party for that title, thought Charles.

"Do you want something to drink?" asked Sam.

"No, it's all right," said Agatha. "How long have you lived in this village?"

"A year. I moved here when my poor husband died."

"Only a year!" exclaimed Agatha. "I was hoping you had been here longer. You can't have had all that much time to get to know the people here very well."

"Ah, but that's where you're wrong. In a place as small as this, you get to know everyone very quickly. What is it that they say? An outsider sees most of the game. I'll surprise you yet. I've got my eye on some-one."

"Then you should tell us or the police," said Agatha. "If the murderer hears of your suspicions, you won't last long."

"Oh, no one would dream of touching me. As a matter of fact, they're all rather in awe of me."

"Why on earth should they be?" asked Charles.

"Very feudal here. Yes, my lady, no, my lady." She gave a modest smile.

Fred walked in. "Going to the pub."

"Don't you have things to do?"

"Like drinking, yes."

Fred turned and walked out. Sam gave a deprecating little smile and then sighed. "My dears, the help these days!"

They questioned her further, but she kept saying she had nothing really to tell them. Agatha had a strong feeling she was holding something back.

As she and Charles walked back to the pub, Agatha said, "I don't know how Sam can bear to have someone like Fred around."

"Maybe he's a relative," said Charles.

"What!"

"That accent of Sam's is more Royal College of Dramatic Art than upper class. Bet she was an actress."

"How much?"

"Fifty pounds."

"You're on," said Agatha. "I think she's the real thing."

Agatha went up to her room in the pub, seized her notebook computer and carried it down to the garden to join Charles. She switched on the computer, went to Google and typed in Sam's name. She stared at the result on the screen.

"Well?" demanded Charles.

"Okay. You win. Was an actress, Samantha Wilkes, before she married. Parts on various television shows including *Morse*. Snakes and bastards." Agatha opened her wallet and reluctantly paid over fifty pounds. "Buy me a drink at least," she said. "How did you guess? I mean, to look at her now, you'd never think she'd once been attractive."

"Just instinct," said Charles, not wanting to explain that in these dying days of the class system, the county had a fine ear tuned for fakes, knowing that such an explanation would appear as snobbish as it actually was.

That evening, Sam was performing one of what she considered her more tiresome duties as lady of the manor. She was reading to old Mrs. Tripp. She sighed as she picked up the book. Like a lot of people of low self-worth, Sam was only happy when playing a role, but this act, she thought, was wearing thin. She missed London, the noise and the bustle. Fred was her late husband's cousin. Fred had been devoted to her husband. They had both been members of the Communist Party in their youth, but Cyril had changed to the Labour Party, saying that was the road to power. Fred had always acted as a sort of valet-cum-butler. When Cyril took his seat in the Lords, Fred told Sam that he was shocked. Where had all their principles gone? On Cyril's death, he had reluctantly agreed to go to Piddlebury with Sam, and, thought Sam, she wished now she had never agreed to the arrangement.

"What are you thinking about?" Mrs. Tripp's voice broke into her thoughts.

"I was thinking about the murders and I'm pretty sure I know who the murderer is."

"And who would that be?"

"I shall make an announcement when I have more evidence," said Sam.

"Fiddlesticks. You going to read or what? It's a new one."

Sam picked up a copy of *The Duke's Desire* and began to read.

"Courtney Winter was a saucy wench, or that is how everyone in the top ten thousand described her. She had a heart-shaped face . . ." Sam raised her eyes from the page. "Why do they always have heart-shaped faces?"

"Blessed if I know. Go on."

After she had gone, Mrs. Tripp picked up the book and began to read. She had good eyesight but liked the idea of people thinking they were doing their community duty by reading to her.

After a time, Mrs. Tripp decided to take a short walk before going to bed. She met Mrs. Pound, the vicarage cleaner, a short distance from her cottage.

"Got a bit o' gossip for you," said Mrs. Tripp.

"Go on, then," said Mrs. Pound.

"Lady Sam says she knows the name of the murderer."

"Go on with you!"

"Fact."

"Well, I never."

Mrs. Pound "did" for several other houses in the village apart from the vicarage. By the end of the following day, the news that Sam was going to expose the murderer was all over the village.

The news reached Agatha and Charles after a long day interviewing several people and not getting any further.

"Silly woman," said Agatha angrily. "I don't suppose she has the slightest idea. I only hope the murderer doesn't believe her or it will be goodbye Sam."

"Do you think we ought to warn her?" asked Charles.

"Waste of time. She's not going to listen to us and she's not going to admit she hasn't a clue."

"Have you ever stopped to think you might be next on the murderer's list, Aggie?"

"Don't call me Aggie! No, unfortunately, I feel sure our murderer realises I haven't a clue either."

"Look, Agatha," said Charles. "I think I'll pack my bags and clear off. You're used to these days of trekking around questioning people over and over again, but I find it a bit tedious."

They were sitting in the pub garden. To Charles's surprise, Agatha said mildly, "Yes, it must be boring for you." Then he saw her face light up as Brian walked into the garden and realised Agatha wanted him out of the way.

Charles's road home on the following day took him through Mircester. On impulse, he parked in the square and went up to Agatha's office. Only Simon was there, moodily typing out a report. "Where is everyone?" asked Charles.

"Out on jobs," said Simon. "And Mrs. Freedman's gone home with a headache."

"I've been down at Piddlebury with Agatha," said Charles. "It might be a good idea if one of you were to suggest going down there. I don't like the idea of her being on her own."

"I'll suggest it to Patrick."

"Why not yourself?"

"Well, this is in confidence, mind. I want to be around to keep an eye on Toni."

"Why?"

"She's got a new boyfriend—that is if you can call someone as old as him a boy."

"So what's up with him?"

"I haven't found out yet. But she's got into trouble dating older men before. Tell you what, I know she's meeting him for lunch at the George. Why don't you go along and take a look at him?"

"Why don't you?"

"I tried to join them two days ago and she accused me of spying on her."

"Oh, I suppose I could do with a bit of lunch."

Charles saw Toni as soon as he walked into the dining room. The man with her was seated with his back to the dining room entrance. Toni saw Charles and waved.

Toni was not in her usual jeans and T-shirt. She was

wearing a cotton dress as blue as her eyes. Her naturally blond hair gleamed with health. Despite her detective job, thought Charles, she always looks so fresh and innocent. He walked up to her table.

"Charles," said Toni. "Let me introduce you. This is Luke . . ."

"Fairworth," said Charles. "How are you getting on, Luke?"

Luke Fairworth was a tall, good-looking man, impeccably tailored and barbered. He had black hair and black eyes, a prominent nose and a small mouth.

"You know each other?" exclaimed Toni.

"Luke is the master of the Cheevely Hunt," said Charles. "They meet at my place once a year. Mind if I join you?"

"Please do," said Toni.

Charles sat down and a waiter rushed forward to lay another place setting.

"How's the family?" asked Charles. "Let me see, your daughter must be about Toni's age by now." He guessed Luke must be in his early forties.

"Hardly," said Luke crossly.

"And the wife?"

"I'm divorced."

"How sad. When did that happen?"

"Last year. Can we talk about something else? How do you know Toni?"

"I'm a friend of her boss and also a close friend of hers. I've just got back from Piddlebury, Toni."

"Oh, the poisoning case. What's been happening?"

Charles ordered a steak and baked potato, helped himself to wine, and began to tell Toni all about the murders while Luke scowled.

At last, Luke glanced at his watch. "I've got to run. I'll see you this evening, Toni." He called the waiter. "Separate bills," he said.

When Luke had paid up and left, Charles asked curiously, "Does he never pay for your lunch?"

"He's a bit short at the moment," said Toni.

"Of course his children's schooling must take a bit," said Charles.

"Children!"

"Yes, there's Mark, he must be sixteen by now. Nearly your age. Emma is twelve and Olivia, eight."

"You're making this up!" exclaimed Toni.

"Not I. I remember his divorce now. Cruelty, wasn't it?"

"His wife's?"

"No, his."

"I don't believe you."

"You'd better apply your detective skills to the Internet," said Charles. "More wine?"

Toni stood up. "Agatha is always interfering in my

personal life and I know she's sent you to do just that. Sorry, Charles. Your very colourful lies just won't work."

Toni stormed off. Blast Luke, thought Charles. Now I'm the one who's got to pay for her lunch.

Toni switched on her computer in the office and put in Luke's name. Nothing there. Charles must be lying. But she could not leave it alone. She went round to the local newspaper's offices to see a reporter friend, Jimmy Swift.

"I want details of a divorce case that happened, oh, about a year ago."

"Name?"

"Just his. Luke Fairworth."

"It'll take a bit of time. Help yourself to coffee."

Toni collected a mug of coffee from a machine in the corner and then stood at the window overlooking Market Street. The market was busy, people clustered round the stalls. Striped awnings over the stalls moved lazily in the lightest of breezes.

"Got it!" called Jimmy.

Toni went to join him.

"Hang on," he said. "I'll print it off."

She waited impatiently as the office's old laser printer slowly churned out page after page.

He handed her six pages. Toni snatched them, said a brief "thanks" and hurried out of the office.

She went to an open-air café in the main square, ordered an iced coffee and began to read.

Her heart plummeted as she read the pages. The divorce was granted on the grounds of Luke's cruelty. Mrs. Sarah Fairworth had been granted custody of the children. There were reports of the police having been called to their home on several occasions to find Mrs. Fairworth had suffered from a beating. She had refused to press charges. But evidence from her doctor and evidence from the local hospital where she had been admitted for a broken arm on one occasion and cracked ribs on another gave her lawyers the proof they needed. Nobody loves the messenger and Toni wondered whether she could ever speak to Charles again. She felt very young and very silly.

Charles had phoned Agatha with the news. "I hope he doesn't get violent when she dumps him," said Agatha. "She's got holiday owing. I'll see if I can get her to take it now."

But Toni refused. She was proud of the fact that Agatha left the running of the agency to her while she was away. She had already phoned Luke to say that she wouldn't be seeing him again, to which he replied that he would like to break Charles Fraith's neck. He went on trying to explain that his wife had made the whole thing up. Toni interrupted with a quiet and firm "good-bye."

Simon had entered the office while she was phoning. He stood quietly in the doorway listening, and then he grinned happily. There was hope for him yet.

Chapter Four

Agatha was thinking of returning to Mircester. She called on Jerry Tarrant to explain that there was little she could do with police and press all over the place but that she would return when things had quietened down.

Her idea of departure was speeded by the fact that Brian Summer was no longer staying at the inn. He had decided to spend the school holidays in Piddlebury and so he had taken a room at Mrs. Ada White's farmhouse. She found it odd that he should want to stay with so many press around, one of whom might tie his name to that poisoning in Oxford.

Besides, he had started to avoid her. She had seen him out walking and had hurried to join him but just when she had caught up with him, he had said, "Must rush," and had fled into the woods like a startled deer.

The glorious weather had broken at last, not in any dramatic thunderstorm but in a damp mist shrouding the countryside, turning Piddlebury into a sort of ghost village where shapes came and went in the mist like so many wraiths.

Agatha made a last call on Sam and lectured her on the folly of saying she knew the identity of the murderer and therefore putting herself at risk.

"I can look after myself," said Sam. She was wearing scarlet lipstick on her mouth surrounded by thin wrinkles. It gave her mouth the appearance of looking like a badly stitched wound. She smokes, thought Agatha. That's the reason for all those nasty wrinkles. I must give up somehow.

"Well, I'm leaving," said Agatha. "Not much I can do at the moment. I'll give it a few weeks."

She returned to the inn, paid her bill, got into her car and drove off. Despite the mist, the day was muggy and warm. Agatha switched on the air-conditioning. She wrinkled her nose. A really nasty smell was coming through the air vents. She stopped the car, got out and raised the bonnet. Two very dead rats were lying on top of the engine.

She got a pair of latex gloves out of the glove box, picked up the creatures and tossed them off into the grass at the side of the road.

Agatha got behind the wheel again and sat there, irresolute. Should she go back to the inn and ask questions? She had begun locking her car. She had loaded in her suitcase but had gone back to check she had left nothing behind. Wait a bit. Moses had offered her a coffee and she had drunk one quickly in the bar. That must have been when someone put the rats in her car.

She sighed. There was no point in going back, she decided. With the mist, probably no one would have noticed anything. But yet, in a way, it had been a sort of attack. Agatha swung the car round and went back to the mobile police unit in the village.

Bill Wong was just leaving the unit when she arrived. She hailed him and told him about the rats. "I'd better get forensics to go over your car," said Bill. "You go to the inn and I'll tell you when they're finished."

Agatha walked slowly back to the inn. "Hullo again," said Moses.

"Someone put rats in my car, probably when I was

drinking that coffee," said Agatha. "Any idea who might have done it?"

"I've been here all the time," said Moses. "My wife's been making rabbit pie for lunch. You should stay for that."

"May as well," said Agatha. "I'll need to pass the time until a forensic team has gone over my car."

She went into the pub garden. To her surprise, Ada White was sitting at one of the tables, accompanied by a heavyset man.

Agatha approached her. "How's things?"

"Awful," said Ada. "They've taken away all the home-made wine out of my cellar to the lab. It'll be ruined. Oh, this is my husband, Ken."

Ken had thick grey hair and a truculent face. "Leave us alone," he said. "The missus has had enough of questions."

Normally, Agatha would have persisted, but the discovery of the rats had shaken her. She went to another table and sat down.

She brightened when Brian walked in. She waved him over but he smiled, waved back and went to sit at another table, as far away from Agatha as possible.

To pass the time, she phoned Toni, who gave her a brisk rundown on all the cases. Agatha told her about the rats and said she would be returning as soon as her car had been checked.

"And everything all right with you?"

"Why not?" demanded Toni curtly. "See you soon."

Toni was seriously thinking of going for counselling. Luke had not been her first mistake. Was there something wrong with her that she gravitated to much older men with violent tendencies?

The office door opened and James Lacey, Agatha's ex-husband, walked in.

"Agatha is due back from Piddlebury today," said Toni. "She's been on this poisoning case."

"Like to come for lunch?"

Toni hesitated only a moment. Here was one older man who was as safe as houses.

They walked to a Chinese restaurant. Toni told James as much as she knew about Agatha's detecting in Piddlebury, but as she talked, James noticed she looked unhappy.

Over a pot of green tea, he asked gently, "Now, tell me what's upsetting you, Toni."

Toni looked at him. She often thought that Agatha was mad to have let this one get away. James was as handsome as ever with his thick black hair only going a little grey at the temples and his intense blue eyes.

"It's just that I've made another bad mistake," she said slowly.

"A man?"

"Yes."

"A much older man?"

"Yes, again. What's up with me? He turned out to be a wife beater. Do you think I need a psychiatrist?"

"I think that's for you to decide. There are two things to consider. The first is that there are a lot of predatory men around who zoom in on pretty, young girls. Then there are the girls who really want a sort of father figure to admire them, care for them and protect them from this nasty world. What was your own father like?"

"Didn't know him."

"In this wicked world," said James, "the sad fact is that women have to be sure they can take care of themselves. No one else is really going to do it for them. It's best really not to depend on anyone else. There are unfortunates in old folks' homes who believed to the last moment that their sons and daughters would look after them in their old age. If you expect nothing from anybody, you could wake up one day and find yourself in the middle of a genuine and splendid romance." His blue eyes were shining.

"Oh, James," said Toni. "*You've* found someone."

He grinned. "I think I have."

"Who is she?"

"Mary Gotobed."

"You're kidding!"

"I think poor Mary has heard all the jokes there are about her name. It's a good old name."

"Where did you meet her?"

"In Carsely. She's just moved into the village."

"Divorced? Widowed?"

"What a lot of questions you do ask, young Toni. Mary is a widow."

"Got a photo?"

James fished out his wallet and extracted a small photograph. Toni studied the woman in it with surprise. Mary was plain and motherly looking with curly brown hair, a round face and a plump figure.

"What will Agatha think?" asked Toni.

"It's got nothing to do with Agatha. She's always too busy chasing some man or other to bother about what I am doing."

By the time Agatha had retrieved her car, she felt too tired to go to the office and so she drove straight home.

After she had collected her cats from her cleaner, Doris Simpson, she decided to walk up to the vicarage.

"Come in, Mrs. Raisin," said Mrs. Bloxby. "What's been happening in Piddlebury?"

"Two murders and I haven't a clue who did them,"

said Agatha. "I've not given up. I just can't do anything with so many police around. How are things in the village. Anyone new?"

"Just a widow. Rather pleasant. Mary Gotobed."

"Odd name."

"Good old English one. Coffee?"

"Yes, please."

While Mrs. Bloxby poured coffee, she wondered whether to tell Agatha about James's interest in Mary. But Agatha, she knew, was very competitive. With any luck, her work would keep her away from the village.

"Is James back?" asked Agatha when Mrs. Bloxby returned carrying a tray.

"Do have an Eccles cake, Mrs. Raisin. I baked them this morning."

"Maybe just the one."

"I want to hear all about the murders," said Mrs. Bloxby.

So Agatha told her while Mrs. Bloxby listened, grateful that she had diverted her friend's mind from James.

When she had finished, Mrs. Bloxby said, "I am surprised Brian Summer would opt to stay on in the village with so many press around. You would think he would be frightened that someone would dig up that poisoning case in Oxford."

"I think he's a bit odd," said Agatha. "I'd better

phone Patrick. The police must have questioned him along with everyone else in the village. Has James come back?"

"Have another Eccles cake."

Agatha's eyes sharpened. For the first time in their friendship, she thought the vicar's wife looked shifty.

"I asked if James was back."

"I believe so."

"You're trying not to tell me something. Out with it. I may as well hear it from you."

"It's just that James has formed a . . . well, a friend-ship with Mary Gotobed."

"Is she blond and beautiful?"

"No, sort of comfortable and ordinary in a way, but a thoroughly nice woman."

Agatha scowled horribly.

"Now, Mrs. Raisin," said Mrs. Bloxby. "You don't want him so why not let someone else have him?"

"Of course," said Agatha. "You don't think I would interfere, do you?" Her bearlike eyes bored into the mild eyes of Mrs. Bloxby.

"Heaven forbid!" said Mrs. Bloxby, but it sounded more like a prayer than an exclamation.

When Agatha walked back to her cottage, her brain was in turmoil. It was the thought that James might marry someone and be happy with that someone when he had been unhappy with her that riled her.

But Charles arrived that evening. His first remark was, "Heard about James and Mary?"

"Yes," said Agatha curtly.

"Nose out of joint?"

"Don't be silly, Charles. I wish them well."

"Oh, yeah? Well, you're back here. Given up on Piddlebury?"

"I'm waiting until the police give up and I can get a free hand. It's not like the usual Cotswold village these days—full of newcomers. And everyone bitches that it's people like me that have taken the homes away from young villagers. For some reason, there is this myth that newlyweds should be able to walk into a new home. It used to be they lived with one set of parents and saved up and then moved into a bedsit, saved some more, got finally accepted for a council house, or saved up enough for a mortgage. But it's all instant gratification. Besides, either their parents sold their houses to incomers, or, I believe, a good while back, some of the cottages were near ruins, people preferring to move to the cities. Builders bought them up, did them up, started off letting them out as holiday cottages and finally sold them off as homes.

"But Piddlebury is different. It's very small, well off the tourist route. There's a secretive feel to it. Apart from Jerry Tarrant, I'm sure someone knows something and is not telling. Sam Framington claims she knows who did it, but she's one of the few incomers, and I don't believe she has a clue."

"Dangerous thing to do," commented Charles.

"Unless our murderer thinks she's as silly as I do," said Agatha.

Next door, James Lacey was pacing up and down.

"What's the matter?" asked Mary.

"Charles Fraith has just gone in next door with an overnight bag."

"So?"

James sat down suddenly. "I just don't want Agatha getting hurt."

Mary suppressed a flash of irritation. "I'm sure Agatha Raisin is old enough to take care of herself."

"You're right as usual, Mary," said James with a sigh. How relaxing Mary was compared to Agatha. She didn't plaster her face with make-up, or wear ridiculously short skirts and crippling high heels. She didn't smoke like a chimney or run around chasing murderers.

To James's amazement—and the amazement of everyone else in the village—Agatha Raisin left him strictly alone.

Agatha took a brief holiday in the South of France for a week in early August. On her return at the end of the month, she reread her notes on the Piddlebury murders and decided the time had come to get back there. She was also glad of an excuse to leave Carsely, where the romance between James and Mary seemed to be blossoming. Or rather that was what many of the villagers seemed to take delight in telling her.

Agatha decided this time to take Phil Marshall with her. Phil was in his seventies and with his white hair and gentle face he had a knack of getting people to confide in him. She had not seen or heard anything of Charles since his last brief visit.

August had been a dreadful month of pouring rain. But when Agatha and Phil drove up to the pub, each in their separate cars, at the beginning of September, the weather was mellow, sunny and warm.

"What a pretty little gem of a place," said Phil. "Where do we start?"

"We'll dump out suitcases in our rooms," said Agatha, "have a bite of lunch and work out who to interview."

Moses looked surprised and then wary when they walked in, Agatha demanding two rooms.

"I didn't think you'd be back," he said.

"I gather the police aren't around anymore," said Agatha.

"No, we're all settling down again just fine."

"How on earth can you settle down when there's a murderer still on the loose?" exclaimed Agatha.

"The way we look at it is this," said Moses, handing over two brass keys. "It must have been some mad psycho from outside."

Phil saw that Agatha was prepared for a long argument and gave a gentle cough. "I'm sure we can discuss all this later, Agatha."

"Why did you interrupt me?" asked Agatha when they were finally seated in the pub garden.

"Because," said Phil patiently, "you would have been wasting your breath. You were about to point out that a stranger wouldn't have known about the elderberry wine in the cellar or that it was possible to sneak down there and put a bottle of the poisoned stuff in the crate, or that for some reason she would pick that precise time to drink it. Moses had a stubborn look on his face. Where do you want me to start?"

"Try Mrs. Ada White first. And see if you can winkle out of her what Brian Summer was like when he was staying with her. I'll go to the vicarage after I've seen Jerry. I'll phone you if there are any developments."

Jerry welcomed Agatha. "You are going to have a very difficult time," he said.

"More than last time?"

"Oh, yes. Everyone seems to have seized hold of the idea that it must have been someone from outside. There's no longer inbreeding in this village but they all seem to have grabbed hold of the same idea."

"I would have thought someone like, say, Peter Suncliff wouldn't have gone along with the herd."

"I don't know. He's just back from holiday."

"What about our lady of the manor who claims she knows whodunit?"

"As a matter of fact, our Lady Sam is the most vociferous of the outsider psycho solution."

"Odd that. I wonder if she's been got at."

"You don't know this village. If she had been got at, as you put it, everyone would soon know who and why. Also, they are so pleased that they can settle back into their usual ways without suspecting each other and causing a poisonous atmosphere. You will not be popular."

"Do you want me to go on?"

"Yes, certainly."

"I will only bill you for the hours I work."

Jerry put his well-manicured hands together, almost as if praying. "I feel uneasy, nonetheless. I am afraid that when you begin to question everyone all over again, there might be another murder, and I just hope you are not going to be the next victim."

As Agatha made her way to the village, everything seemed to be almost asleep in a rural calm. A pale disk of a sun shone down on the golden stone of the cottages. She was about to pass Gloria's cottage when she noticed the For Sale sign outside and heard sounds of activity. Agatha walked up and rang the bell.

A woman answered the door. "Yes?" she demanded.

"I am Agatha Raisin and I have been employed to find out who killed Gloria French."

"I'm her daughter, Tracey. Come in."

Tracey did not look very much like her mother, being very slim and with a narrow head and small mouth.

"I'm trying to sell off the furniture but one villager or another keeps dropping in to claim back things they say my mother took and didn't give back. Knowing my mother's reputation, I have to believe them. The house clearance people are coming tomorrow. At first I was going to leave everything as it was before I sold the house but villagers seemed to be turning up the whole time to claim things so I decided to get rid of everything."

"Was the house left to you?"

"To me and my brother. We share everything according to the will. The police appear to have given up."

"Oh, they never do and neither do I," said Agatha. "Perhaps you can help me. How could someone know that on that particular morning and at that particular time, your mother would go down to the cellar to look for a drink?"

"She had a bad drinking problem. She was a binge drinker. She could go quite a bit without any and then if something upset her, she would head straight for the bottle."

"I wonder what it was that upset her that particular morning?" said Agatha.

"The vicar called. He said my mother had invited him and his wife for drinks but he made an excuse and before he put the phone down, his wife said, 'Have you managed to put her off?' The vicar was upset about that because he said Mother had done so much for the church and it was awful that the last thing she heard from the vicarage was a snub."

I wonder if Clarice Enderbury knew about Gloria's drinking habits, thought Agatha.

Agatha looked round the room. Her eye fell on a chest of drawers against the wall. Although she knew very little about antiques, Agatha was blessed with a rare instinct for recognising good-quality furniture.

"You're surely never going to let the house clearance people take that chest of drawers away," she said.

"Why? Is it valuable?"

"I think so. I'm no expert."

Agatha went over and examined it. It was of a mellow shade of mahogany with a rectangular top, oval-shaped brass handles and bracket feet.

"I saw something like that last year in an antique shop in Stow-on-the-Wold," said Agatha. "They said it was George the Third and they were asking over a thousand pounds for it. Take a photo of it and show it to Suther's auctioneers in Mircester, but don't let the clearance people get it."

"That is odd," said Tracey. "I mean, Mother never had any taste at all."

"She can't have borrowed it from anyone," said Agatha, "or they would have been around trying to get it back. You took some time to decide to sell the house."

"The police were all over it and I decided to keep out of the way until things were quiet. Wayne, my brother, said he'd leave the arrangements to me."

"Did your mother give you any idea who might have hated her enough to kill her?"

"We didn't speak. She tried to interfere in my marriage. That was five years ago. I told her I never wanted to see her again. Also, she did the dirty on Wayne, selling the business from under him, so he refused to have anything more to do with her."

"And have you and your brother alibis for the day of your mother's death?"

"Of course. I was at the farm and seen by the neighbours. Wayne was at the factory and seen by hundreds of employees during the day. I just wish the murderer could be caught. I won't feel easy until I've got rid of the furniture and then be able to leave this village."

Phil was seated in Ada White's kitchen, drinking coffee and eating sponge cake. Her husband, Ken, had joined them when Phil arrived but had gone back to work.

"It must have been a terrible time for you," said Phil.

Her eyes filled with tears. Phil handed her a clean handkerchief. She dabbed at her eyes. "All those questions from the police! They took away every bottle of my homemade wine and ruined it all in their forensic lab. I'm still waiting for compensation. The police were bad enough but the press were worse. They practically found me guilty. A lawyer from London came to see me and said he would sue the newspapers for me but I just wanted the whole thing to go away."

"I think it might be a good idea to sue them," said Phil. "Did you keep the offending reports?"

"No, I burned them."

"A pity. But I am sure my boss, Mrs. Raisin, can recommend a good lawyer."

"I don't want to go to court!"

"I am sure Mrs. Raisin will track down the murderer, and as soon as that happens, get a lawyer to sue their socks off. You deserve it after all you've been through."

Ada gave him a watery smile. "You're not like a detective at all."

"It helps," said Phil. "Now, have a good think. Who in this village would want to kill Gloria French?"

"Everyone is saying it must have been some madman from outside the village. I wish that were true. There was an awful period when everyone seemed to suspect everyone else. At first everyone liked Gloria. She did so much for the church. She always volunteered to drive elderly people into Mircester for a day's shopping or worked at village fetes. But then she became—how shall I put it?—raucous and pushy. There was a rumour that she drank a lot, but I never saw her drunk and Moses at the pub said she only drank lemonade or some sort of soft drink when she went there. Of course, there was all that business of borrowing things and not giving them back."

"Did she ask you for anything?"

"She wanted to take away a case of elderberry wine from a sale at the church. I told her sharply she'd have to pay for it. At the end of the day, I looked for it. It was a box of six bottles I had kept under the table in the café in reserve in case we ran out. It had gone! I challenged her and she denied it."

"And did people hear you accusing her?"

"Most of the village, I would think."

"What about men?" asked Phil. "Did she have affairs?"

"She tried. She set her cap at the vicar but he was so thrilled with the church repairs that he either didn't notice or pretended not to. His wife loathed Gloria."

"What about Samantha Framington? Didn't she say she knew who the murderer was?"

"She now says she was just joking. Silly sort of joke and a dangerous one. What if the murderer really is in the village?"

"And how did you find Mr. Brian Summer? He stayed with you, I believe."

"He's still here, poor man."

"Not back at school?"

"The press dug up some school poisoning case and the police questioned him over and over again. He got a line from the doctor to say he was suffering from depression and would take a year's sabbatical."

"I would have thought," said Phil, "that he would want to get away from this village."

"He's a thoroughly nice man. We're outside the village here. He likes going for long walks. He says he finds it healing."

Agatha had found no one at home at the vicarage. She tried the church but it was locked. Mrs. Bloxby had told her that the churches had become a target for thieves.

She walked to the village store. Jenny Soper was just leaving. "Oh, you're back!" she exclaimed. "I thought the whole business was over."

"How can it be over when the murderer hasn't been caught?"

She was joined by Peter Suncliff. "Back again?" he said to Agatha.

"Jenny was just saying she thought the whole thing was over," said Agatha. "But how can it be over? Nobody's been caught."

"But nothing has happened since," said Jenny. "Isn't that right, Peter? Doesn't that show it must have been some stranger, some madman?"

"It was too well planned for that," said Agatha. "And any stranger would stand out in a tiny village like this."

"But there are the woods where Craig Upton was poisoned," protested Jenny.

"Craig was poisoned because he stole a bottle of wine from my car," said Agatha. "Have you seen Sam Framington?"

"I saw her earlier, going to the vicarage," said Peter.

Agatha felt suddenly uneasy. Why had there been no reply when she had called at the vicarage?

She said goodbye to the pair and hurried back to the vicarage. Again, there was no reply although she knocked on the door this time as well as ringing the bell.

Agatha stood irresolute. Perhaps they were all in the garden, lying dead. She tried to tell her fertile imagination to shut up, but she told herself it would do no harm to have a look at the back of the vicarage. But the path at the side was blocked by a high, iron padlocked gate, now firmly closed. The church with its graveyard lay next door. Perhaps there was a viewpoint into the garden from the graveyard.

She went into the graveyard and threaded her way through the old mossy gravestones. There was a high stone wall cutting the graveyard off from the vicarage garden next door, but some old tombstones were propped against that wall. Glad that she was wearing flat shoes for once, Agatha hitched up her skirt, grabbed handholds in the old wall and hoisted herself up and peered over the top of the wall.

Sam and Clarice were seated at the garden table on the terrace, sharing a bottle of wine.

Fred came out and said, "I'm off down to the shop and then I'll get back to the manor."

"Right," said Sam. "Are you sure that dreadful detective woman has gone away?"

"Sure as sure. Pushy cow."

In a burst of rage, Agatha heaved herself up to the

top of the wall with such energy that she tumbled over the top and landed on the thick grass in the garden on the other side.

Clarice and Sam were staring at her. Agatha picked herself up, dusted herself down and with a crocodile smile said, "I thought I would just drop in."

"You're trespassing!" exclaimed Clarice. "What the hell are you *doing*?"

"I thought something awful might have happened to you," said Agatha. "I heard, you, Sam, had gone to the vicarage. I mean, last heard you were going about saying you knew the identity of the murderer, so it stands to reason you're a prime target."

"It was just a joke," said Sam shrilly. "I told everyone that."

She's scared, thought Agatha.

"Did anyone threaten you?" she asked.

"No they did not!"

The vicar came out onto the terrace. "Why, Mrs. Raisin, what are you doing standing there? Is there any wine left in that bottle, dear?"

"Mrs. Raisin was just leaving," said Clarice. Her eyes bored into Agatha's face.

"As a matter of fact," said Agatha brightly, "a glass of wine would be very nice." She walked up to the table, pulled out a vacant chair, sat down and smiled all around.

"I'll get you a glass," said Clarice, suddenly transforming back into the character of vicar's wife.

She rose and went indoors.

"I'm off," said Sam, getting to her feet.

"What a pity," said Agatha sweetly. "I've a few questions I wanted to ask you."

"Haven't got the time. Busy, busy, busy." She rushed off.

"Well, Mrs. Raisin," said the vicar. "How is your detecting going?"

Clarice came out with a glass, poured Agatha a little wine and thumped the glass down in front of her.

"Careful, darling," admonished the vicar gently.

"Sorry," mumbled Clarice.

"I am wondering why this village appears to have decided that the murders were committed by some visiting maniac," said Agatha.

The vicar looked surprised. "This is the first I've heard of it. What about you, Clarice?"

"It does seem like the most sensible idea," said Clarice. "I mean, everything's peaceful again and there hasn't been any more trouble."

"I would hardly call murder 'trouble,'" said Agatha.

"Exactly," agreed the vicar. "But what can we do to help?"

Agatha felt frustrated. She turned to Clarice. "You

were round at the back door of Gloria's cottage when she was murdered. Didn't you see anyone at all?"

"What's this?" The vicar looked surprised. "I had already cancelled our visit to her."

"I just suddenly wanted to get our Crown Derby bowl back," said Clarice, shooting a venomous look at Agatha. "I told you I heard noises and thought she was having sex with someone."

"My dear! Why didn't you tell me this? And do the police know?"

"I didn't want to get involved," said Clarice. "I mean, I didn't see anyone or hear anything apart from those odd noises."

"But you might have been able to save her," exclaimed the vicar. "And what on earth made you think she was having sex of all things?"

"She was always chasing one man or another," said Clarice sulkily. "The way she came on to you, Guy, was a disgrace."

Her husband looked genuinely shocked. "I'm sure you must have imagined it," he said. "I never noticed anything."

"You never do," said Clarice bitterly.

Agatha decided wearily that she was not going to hear anything of interest no matter how long she stayed, but she did beg Clarice to think again and see if she could remember anything.

Outside, she phoned Phil, who said he had just arrived back at the pub and was in the garden if she would like a report.

She hurried back and found him sitting under the shade of an elm tree, sipping lemonade.

When he told her that Brian Summer was still in the village and still staying with Ada White, Agatha brightened up. Although she would not admit it to herself, she was constantly searching for something to take her mind off James and Mary back in Carsely.

Mary was away visiting relatives in Deale and James had an interview with the local paper. He hated interviews and yet he knew it was wise to publicise his books as much as possible. When he left the newspaper, he decided to call at the detective agency and see if Toni might be free for dinner. He felt she needed cheering up. It was seven in the evening, but he knew Toni often worked late.

Toni was there, and said she would be delighted. Simon was also at his desk and as Toni and James left, James turned round and found Simon scowling at him.

He hesitated on the stairs leading down from the office. "Maybe I should go back and ask Simon to join us."

"No, please," said Toni. "I'm with Simon most of the day and that's long enough."

"Where would you like to eat?"

"It's still lovely weather. Anywhere we can sit outdoors."

"The George Hotel has some tables out on the terrace. Let's see if we can get one."

Soon they were seated out in the terrace, looking out over the hotel garden at the back.

After they had ordered their food, Toni sat back in her chair with a sigh. "This is so kind of you. Perhaps I should have gone home and changed into something a bit smarter."

"You look fine," said James, and meant it. Toni's blond hair had grown long and was worn loose. She was wearing a blue denim blouse which matched her eyes, a short denim skirt and low-heeled sandals.

"How's Mary?" asked Toni.

"Gone to visit relatives. I've just endured a newspaper interview and I felt like relaxing. How's Agatha getting on?"

"She's gone back to Piddlebury with Phil. I haven't had a report from her yet."

"Had any trouble from Luke?"

"None at all. I can't understand it. I'm a pretty good detective and I'm good at sizing up people, except when it comes to older men."

"Well, if you find yourself gravitating to another one, bring him along to see Daddy James and I'll look him over for you."

"Thanks. I'll do that."

"Tell me what cases you've got at the moment?" asked James.

Toni talked on during the meal. James watched her and thought he was not surprised that mature men fell for her. She was fresh and pretty.

As she talked, Toni thought that James was really very attractive with his bright blue eyes in his tanned face. Somehow, they both lingered over their coffee, reluctant to end the evening.

At last Toni said, "Thanks for dinner. It's been great. When does Mary get back?"

"Not soon enough," said James. "She's supposed to run the tombola stand at the village fete on Saturday and it looks as if I'll have to do it."

"I tell you what," said Toni, "I'll come along and help you."

"Would you? That would be great."

Simon stared blindly at the television screen in his flat. He longed to phone Agatha and tell her that James had taken Toni out for dinner. But Toni would be furious and so would James. Still, he'd keep an eye on Toni.

Agatha saw Peter Suncliff seated at another table and went over to talk to him. "What now?" he asked.

"It turns out that Gloria had a drinking problem but she was a binge drinker and only went for the bottle when she was upset. Now, on the morning of the murder, apart from the confrontation with Jenny, was there anything else? Did anyone else upset her?"

"There was old Mrs. Tripp," said Peter reluctantly. "She said something nasty to Jenny that Jenny was at the menopause and Mrs. Tripp weighed in with something like Jenny was too young but Gloria was not. I can't remember the whole thing."

Agatha went back to join Phil and told him what Peter had said. "Right," said Phil, "we should go and see her."

Agatha knew that the old lady would probably demand a reading from one of her romances first. "You go," she said to Phil. "I'm sure you'll have the gentler touch."

"And what will you do?"

"I'll go over my notes and see if there is anything we missed."

"All right," said Phil, but wondering why Agatha looked shifty.

Agatha watched Phil as he walked away. He was

dressed for the heat in a grey cotton shirt and grey chinos. His white hair was thick and looked healthy. Remarkable for his age, thought Agatha, and then remembered gloomily that Phil did not smoke and drank sparingly.

"You're that other detective," said Mrs. Tripp, after she had opened the door to Phil. "Come in."

Phil went into her cluttered living room. "Sit down," she ordered, "and read to me."

"I would like to ask you a few questions," said Phil.

"Read first."

She handed him a paperback called *Deborah's Desire.* "Page fifty," she ordered.

Phil felt trapped. The small room was hot. Sun flickered on the silver frames of the many photographs.

He opened the book and began to read. "The Marquess of Dulwater brooded over the cringing figure of Deborah. 'Kiss me!' he ordered. 'I cannot,' she sobbed. 'You are taking advantage of me because I am poor.'"

Snore.

Phil looked up from the book. Mrs. Tripp had fallen asleep. He rose to leave. She opened her eyes. "Have you read?" she demanded.

"Pages and pages," said Phil, hoping she believed him.

"Sit down," she said. "What do you want to know?"

"Have you any idea who committed these murders?"

"I tell you, it was some nut case from outside the village."

"But you said before," said Phil, consulting his notes, "that the vicar's wife was guilty."

"I thought she was but I was wrong."

"Look," said Phil patiently, "how could someone from outside the village get hold of Mrs. White's elderberry wine and change it for a mixture of poison from rhubarb leaves and soda?"

"These maniacs can be right clever."

"Suppose it turns out to be someone from the village. Have you any suggestion as to who it might be?"

"No, and you're wasting your time. And be glad o' that! Think on. If this murderer is someone in the village, then you're next." She gave a cackle of laughter and sent a blast of foul breath in Phil's direction.

Agatha had figured out that if Brian Summer went out walking, he would probably walk in the woods. She drove to the edge of the woods, got out of her car, and set off on foot. She was grateful for the cool greenness.

She had not expected to have much success in finding him but felt that any activity was better than none.

If she did not come across him, then she would go to the farm and see if Mrs. White would let her wait for him.

After half an hour, Agatha began to think of the walk back and was just about to turn around when the trees opened up into a clearing and there, sitting on a fallen log, reading a book, was Brian Summer. He looked up and saw her, scrambled to his feet and stood poised for flight.

"I wondered why you had decided to stay on in the village," said Agatha, advancing on him.

He sank down miserably back on the log. Agatha sat down beside him. He was as attractive as she had remembered him to be with his tall, lean body and thick white hair.

"After all the police questions, I suffered from depression. The police dug up all that stuff about the teenager dying at that party. You know about that?"

"Yes."

"A doctor signed me off. It's peaceful here. It's one of the last villages in the Cotswolds which seems cut off from the outside world."

"But here! Why here of all places? Two unsolved murders."

"I felt I of all people had nothing to fear from the murderer."

"Why?"

"I did not know Gloria French. I have no idea who might be the murderer."

He was wearing shorts. Agatha cast a covert eye at his strong, muscular legs.

"Why don't we have dinner this evening?" she suggested brightly.

"How very kind of you." He rose to his feet with one fluid movement. "But I really prefer my own company at the moment."

"Well, goodbye, Greta Garbo," muttered Agatha to the uncaring trees as Brian strode away and was soon lost to sight.

Phil was arriving back from Mrs. Tripp's house as she returned to the inn. "I haven't had any luck," he said. "She really doesn't have the faintest idea. She's just a silly old woman. And she smells."

"I didn't have any luck with Brian either," said Agatha, thinking, In more ways than one. "Let's have some tea and figure out which one to talk to next."

Over tea in the garden, they consulted their notes. "I think we should have a joint go at Sam," said Agatha. "I feel she's holding something back."

They finished their tea and walked along to the

manor. "It's the village fete in Carsely today," said Phil. "They have good weather for it."

James and Toni were working happily together at the tombola stand. "We've a better lot of prizes this year," said James. "Usually they just recycle the rubbish they won the year before. Buy a ticket, Mrs. Arnold?"

Carsely's most spiteful resident bought a ticket and Toni spun the wheel. "You've got a prize," she said. "Number 83."

"Nothing but a tin of sardines," grumbled Mrs. Arnold. "Cheapskates."

Simon watched Toni from behind a secondhand book stand. She was wearing her blond hair loose on her shoulders and it gleamed in the sunlight. She was laughing at something James was saying. The brief shorts she was wearing showed off her long tanned legs and she had a white shirt knotted at the waist.

They seemed to be enjoying each other's company. Thank goodness James is so old, thought Simon. He guessed James must be in his early fifties and Toni was not yet twenty. Then he remembered Toni's penchant for older men but shrugged it off. James had always been like an uncle to Toni.

He did not want to be caught lurking around. He

decided to go back to Mircester. Toni parked her car in the square. He would wait there at the end of the day and see if she would join him for a drink.

Mrs. Bloxby, serving at the cake stand, felt uneasy as she watched James and Toni. Toni, she knew, was totally unaware of her beauty. She suddenly wished that Mary Gotobed would return to the village very soon.

At the end of the day, James said, "Well, we've got rid of practically everything. The vicar is acting as treasurer. I'll take the money over to him. Do you want to push off?"

"I'll help you pack up the stand," said Toni. "I've still got time."

"Heavy date this evening?"

"Just with myself," said Toni. "There's a showing of *The Artist,* that French film, at the arts cinema."

"I never saw that," said James. "Tell you what, I'll take you as a thanks and then we can have a bite to eat afterwards."

Simon saw Toni drive up and park in the square. To his dismay, James parked his car next to hers. They both got out and walked off together. Simon followed them. He saw them go into the arts cinema. He thought of buying a ticket, but realised, if Toni saw him, she might guess he was checking up on her.

He went back to the office instead. He sat down at his computer and sent an e-mail to Agatha. "Everything quiet here. How are you getting on? Toni and James worked the tombola stand at the fete in Carsely together and have now gone to a movie. Nice to see him looking after her. Simon."

Agatha and Phil returned to the manor. They had tried earlier without success. This time, Fred answered the door. He stared at them for a long moment, shrugged and walked away into the manor. But he left the door open. After a little hesitation, Agatha and Phil followed him in. They could hear Fred's voice in the drawing room, "That dirty old cow is back," and Sam's petulant reply, "Couldn't you have got rid of her?"

Agatha walked into the drawing room, followed by Phil. "What is it now?" demanded Sam. "I'm tired of answering questions."

"I have a feeling you know something," said Agatha. "Something you're not telling us."

"If I knew anything at all, I'd have told the police. I have nothing more to say to you," said Sam. "Shove off."

"I still think she knows something," fretted Agatha. "Oh, well, let's have dinner and plan a campaign for tomorrow."

Agatha went up to her room first to fetch a jacket because the evening was becoming chilly. The leaves on the trees outside her bedroom window were turning gold at the edges, a herald of autumn, bad weather, dark nights, and thoughts of old age to one private detective.

She took her small notepad computer down to the restaurant. "What's on the menu?" she asked Phil.

"Usual pub grub," said Phil, "except they do have steak and kidney pie this evening. Don't you want to move inside? It's not warm anymore."

"I like the fresh air," said Agatha. "I'll have the pie and a glass of red wine." She lit a cigarette and switched on her computer.

Agatha read the e-mail from Simon and scowled horribly. "Toni worked with James at the tombola," she said to Phil, "and then he took her out for a movie and dinner."

"Mary's away at the moment," said Phil. "Nothing wrong with that. It's young Simon I'm worried about. He must have been stalking her."

But Agatha was worried. She knew young Toni's

weakness for older men. But James would never . . . would he?

Her thoughts were interrupted by a siren racing past outside. Agatha ran out of the pub, followed by Phil. An ambulance followed by a police car was screeching to a stop outside old Mrs. Tripp's cottage. A group of villagers had gathered outside.

The vicar's wife was standing there, her face white. "What's happened?" asked Agatha.

"She wanted me to read to her," said Clarice. "As I was leaving, she asked me to pour her a glass of that dreadful chocolate liqueur that she likes. I did that and then I left. I was just at the gate when I heard these terrible noises. I ran inside again. She was groaning and holding her stomach and the smell was awful. I phoned the ambulance."

"Why weren't you inside trying to help?" asked Agatha.

"I c-couldn't," she stammered. "I didn't know wh-what to do. I h-had to get out of there. That awful smell."

The crowd fell silent as Mrs. Tripp was carried out on a stretcher. She looked as small as a child.

A policewoman approached Clarice. "I must ask you to come with us."

"But my husband . . ."

"I'll tell Guy," said Agatha.

As his wife was being driven off and a forensic team arrived followed by Wilkes, Alice and Bill Wong, the vicar came hurrying up.

Agatha approached him. "Your wife's been taken off for questioning," she said.

"But, why? What's been happening here?"

Agatha told him. "I must go to headquarters immediately," said Guy Enderbury. "My poor wife."

Agatha waited and waited until a thin new moon rose above the village and the crowd grew thicker. "Reckon it be that poisoner again," said someone and a little frisson of shock ran through the watchers.

Somewhere amongst this crowd is a murderer, thought Agatha. She covertly studied the faces although it was hard to see in the dark. Much to the fury of the police, a television crew arrived and soon the scene was lit with blue light. They were told to dismantle their equipment and clear off, but while the scene was brightly lit, Agatha's eyes moved quickly from one face to another. Sam and Fred were on the outskirts, their faces impassive. Jenny was standing close to Peter Suncliff as if for support. Jerry Tarrant approached Agatha.

"This is dreadful," he said. "At least it might show this lot that we are surely dealing with someone from the village."

Alice Peterson came up to join them. "Mr. Marshall," she said. "I hear you were seen entering Mrs. Tripp's cottage earlier. We are going back to headquarters to leave the forensic team to do their work. You must come with us to headquarters."

"Go on," said Agatha to Phil. "I'll follow you."

Agatha parked in the square outside police headquarters. She phoned Patrick and told him the latest news. "See if you can find out quickly what sort of poison she was given," said Agatha. "I know it takes time but usually they have some initial idea."

She rang off and was about to get out of her car when she suddenly saw James and Toni, crossing the square. Toni was laughing at something James had said and he was looking down at her with an indulgent smile on his face. The little scene was lit by the tall lamps surrounding the car park.

Agatha had been about to go and confront them but she suddenly sank back in the driver's seat. Oh, dear, she thought. What on earth does James think he is doing?

The couple reached the corner of the square and turned off down one of the cobbled lanes, leading to Toni's flat. Forgetting all about Phil, Agatha got out and set off in pursuit.

Toni's flat was on the first floor of an old building. Agatha stood in the darkness between two streetlamps on the other side of the road and looked up at Toni's living room window.

The light came on illuminating James saying something. Toni appeared with a bottle of wine and two glasses. Then they disappeared from view, obviously having sat down.

Agatha felt a jumble of intense emotions sweeping through her: loneliness, jealousy and worry.

Then she remembered why she was in Mircester. I must think of something I can do, she thought. James is being silly.

At police headquarters, she took a seat in the reception area and sent an e-mail to Charles. "Help," she wrote. "It looks as if James is romancing Toni. Do you know anything about it? Can we do anything? Love, Agatha."

After half an hour of waiting, her phone rang. Patrick's voice came on the line. "I'm at the hospital," he said. "I pretended I was visiting a relative and went to the corridor where the old girl's room was. A policeman on duty knew me. I asked what was up with her and he said she had been given a huge dose of laxative. I said they'd found that out pretty quickly and he said that they seemed pretty sure."

"Must be Clarice, the vicar's wife," said Agatha.

"They think she must be the murderer."

"Seems odd that a poisoner should only give the old girl a laxative," said Agatha.

"Well, Mrs. Tripp is old and the dehydration could have killed her."

"But Clarice phoned for an ambulance."

"If I find out any more, I'll get back to you," said Patrick and rang off.

The vicar arrived and demanded to see his wife. He was accompanied by a lawyer. He was ushered through into the nether regions of headquarters.

After half an hour, Phil appeared. "What a grilling!" he exclaimed. "You would think I had done it."

Agatha told him what Patrick had said.

"That's odd," commented Phil. "If she really meant to kill her, she surely would have slipped something stronger into her drink and then she would have cleared off and not called for an ambulance."

"Now she's got a lawyer, I don't think they can hold her," said Agatha. "Unless she confesses, I doubt if there would be any proof that she actually gave Mrs. Tripp the laxative. The old girl may have taken the stuff herself and overdid it."

Agatha phoned Patrick again. "Did you find out whether Mrs. Tripp took the laxative herself?"

"Not yet. I'll try in the morning."

The hours passed. Outside, the sky began to lighten.

Phil had fallen asleep. But Agatha was too churned up with thoughts of James and Toni to sleep.

At last Clarice appeared, red-eyed with weeping and supported by her husband. The vicar curtly refused a lift in a police car and said their lawyer would drive them home.

"Clarice," began Agatha, approaching her.

"Leave me alone!" shouted Clarice as she was hustled out of police headquarters by her husband and lawyer. The reception area was suddenly lit with flashes of light from the press cameras outside.

Phil, now awake, said, "What shall we do?"

"You go to the hospital, say you're her nephew, and get in to see her."

"Won't work," said Phil. "She was never married. The cop on duty will go and tell her that her nephew has called, she'll say she hasn't a nephew and then I'll be in trouble."

"Oh well," sighed Agatha, "back to the village. What a waste of a night."

They emerged from police headquarters. The press had gone. Agatha suddenly stood stock-still on the steps. James Lacey was crossing the square to his car.

Agatha ran straight across to him. James heard her coming and swung round in surprise. "Why, Agatha! What . . . ?"

That was as far as he got because Agatha smacked

him full across the face. James seized her arms and pinned them behind her back. "What the hell has got into you?" he demanded.

"You spent the night with Toni," yelled Agatha.

"I spent the night in Toni's flat on the sofa because I had been drinking and wanted to sober up before I drove home. Furthermore, what business is it of yours?"

"You know Toni's weakness for older men. You are trying to seduce her."

"I am trying to get out of here so that I can go home and shower and shave and then I am going to propose marriage to Mary Gotobed when she returns this morning."

He released Agatha and stood back. "In future, mind your own business."

"Come along," said Phil quietly, tugging at Agatha's arm.

Agatha let him lead her back to her car. She suddenly felt tired and old and wanted to cry.

Later that morning, James, spruced up and with a diamond ring in his pocket, went to pick up Mary and take her to a restaurant in Broadway. When he saw her again, he felt a stab of surprise. A treacherous thought entered his head that Mary looked, well, dowdy.

He had told her it was to be a special lunch and yet she had not put on any make-up and was wearing a droopy grey cardigan over a faded green blouse and a wool skirt that dipped at the hem.

In the restaurant in Broadway, James shook out his napkin and looked out of the window. It was beginning to rain, a fine, soaking drizzle.

"I hope you brought an umbrella," he said to Mary.

She patted her tight helmet of curls with a complacent hand. "I had a feeling this was a special occasion," she said, "so I went to the hairdresser. I've got one of those plastic hoods in my bag. Now, what have you been up to since I've been away?"

"Nothing much," said James, trying to banish an image of Toni's glowing face. How awful, he thought. I've become an old lecher. I must not see her again.

They chose their food. Mary talked amiably about her elderly mother—remarkable for her age—while James tried to fight down a feeling of being trapped.

It's all Agatha's fault, thought James. She got me used to dramatic ups and downs and adventure.

He could feel the ring in his pocket. When he escorted Mary out to his car, she put on her plastic hood. He could tell she was disappointed in him.

But the ring stayed in his pocket.

———

After catching up on sleep, Agatha and Phil met up to discuss what to do next.

"I'm sure we haven't a hope of getting near Clarice," said Agatha. "She and Sam seem to be pretty close."

"She'll probably get the awful Fred to say she isn't at home."

"True. But we'll park a little way away from the manor and see if she comes out."

"Agatha, can I say something?"

"If it's about James Lacey, forget it!" snapped Agatha.

They walked out of the inn and got into Agatha's car and drove the little distance to just before the entrance to the manor. Agatha parked under the shelter of a large sycamore. "Rain," she said bleakly. "I suppose the good weather couldn't last forever."

"There goes Fred," said Phil. "No, you don't need to hide. He's walking the other way."

"Now he's out of the road," said Agatha, "we may as well see if she answers the door herself."

They rang and knocked and waited. At last the door opened and Sam surveyed them. She half made to close the door and then gave a little shrug. "Come in."

They all sat down in the drawing room. "Now what?" demanded Sam.

"I feel you know something—that you are holding something back," said Agatha. "I asked you about this before."

"Oh, do give up!" exclaimed Sam. "I don't know a thing."

"Were you near Mrs. Tripp's cottage before she fell ill?" asked Phil.

His mild voice and manner seemed to have a calming effect on Sam. "No, but is she dead?"

"No," said Phil. "It appears someone put a strong dose of laxative in her drink."

"Really? Well, she always was an old shit," said Sam and began to laugh.

"It's no laughing matter," said Agatha severely. "At her age, it could have killed her."

"Well, I had nothing to do with it. Probably some villager who got tired of being trapped reading to her."

"Do you think Clarice might have had something to do with it?" pursued Agatha. "You are her friend, are you not?"

"Yes, I am, and I'm sorry for her. It's hell being a vicar's wife in a small village, being used as a dogsbody by everybody."

Chapter Five

Wat we need to find out," said Agatha the following day, "is if it was generally known that
Gloria was a binge drinker. Also, someone would also
need to be aware of her pattern of drinking—that she
fled to the bottle when she was upset. This village is
getting me down."

Agatha's phone rang. It was Toni. "We're suddenly
getting a bit overloaded with work here," said Toni.
"Any chance of you coming back?"

Agatha wished with all her heart she could just walk
away from this case. But returning meant facing Toni

and worrying about James. "Give me some more time," said Agatha. "I'll send Phil back."

After she rang off, she said to Phil, "That was Toni. We seem to have a lot of work and they always need a photographer. Why don't you leave? It only takes one of us to ferret around this peasant-ridden hellhole."

After Phil had packed and left, Agatha stayed on in the pub garden over a cooling cup of black coffee. The weather had turned fine again and sunlight flickered through the leaves of the trees which shaded the garden, casting moving shadows over Agatha's worried face as she scanned her notes.

Her thoughts were interrupted by Moses Green. "You have a visitor, Mrs. Raisin. I didn't tell him you were here in case it was someone you didn't want to see."

"Who is it?"

"A Mr. Roy Silver."

"Oh, he's all right. Send him through."

Roy once worked for Agatha when she ran her own public relations firm. When he entered the pub garden, Agatha stared at him in amazement. Despite the warmth of the day, he was wearing a flat tweed cap, a hacking jacket over a Tattersall shirt, knee breeches, lovat socks and brogues.

"Who on earth are you supposed to be?" demanded Agatha.

"It's my country look," said Roy huffily.

"It's not you at all. What brings you?"

"I've got a week's holiday." Roy sat down in a chair opposite her and pulled off his cap and mopped his rather weak face with a silk handkerchief. "I thought I'd help you detect. Are the press around?"

"No," said Agatha with a malicious smile, knowing Roy's craving for personal publicity. "Your journey was not necessary. What have you been working on?"

"I've been drumming up publicity for Country Air."

"What on earth is that?"

"It's a new fragrance for men. Husky and redolent of the outdoors."

"Any success?"

"Lots. Hence the time off. I wore this outfit to the launch, sweetie, and I tell you, it was much admired. But you're right. Wait here while I change."

Roy appeared half an hour later in a pink shirt, denim shorts, and trainers. He had a gold medallion nestling in the hair on his chest.

"I gather that hair is stuck on," said Agatha.

"It looks real," said Roy petulantly. "Are you going to fill me in on these murders or sit there nit-picking?"

Agatha, glad of an excuse to clear her thoughts, went over everything she knew.

"The one you don't seem to have an interview with is the vicar, Enderbury. Why not?"

"Seems an unlikely candidate."

"Why? Just because he's a reverend? Hidden fire in some of these church folk. I remember a curate . . ."

"Spare me. Okay. Have it your way. We'll drop along to the vicarage."

"Odd sort of place," commented Roy as they emerged from the pub. "Doesn't look as if time has touched it."

"Well, murder has."

"How's James?"

"Why do you ask?" demanded Agatha sharply.

"I called in at Carsely first. All over the village is the news that James has dumped a sterling female called Mary Gotobed—only she didn't. Get it?" Roy cackled and did two cartwheels along the road.

"Stop acting the clown," said Agatha crossly. "If you're going to help me detect, try to act like a detective."

Mrs. Pound, the vicarage cleaner, answered the door and said the vicar was in the church.

They walked to the church and pushed open the door. Despite the warmth of the day outside, the church was cold and smelled of incense and damp hassocks. It was a Gothic revival building with beautiful stained-glass windows. The vicar was kneeling before the altar, his head bent in prayer.

Agatha coughed loudly. Guy Enderbury looked around and got reluctantly to his feet.

He walked towards them, demanding harshly, "What is it now?"

"Just a few questions," said Agatha.

"You saw I was at prayer," said Guy. "There is no respect these days. I blame the slap-happy type of service that is ruining the Church of England. Do you know the meaning of the word 'awe'?"

Agatha shuffled her feet and looked embarrassed. Guy fixed Roy with a piercing eye. "And what about you, young man? Come on. What do you know about the word 'awe'?"

Roy tittered and began to sing in a high falsetto, "Aw, dear, what can the matter be / Two old ladies locked in the lavatory."

"It is not a joking matter. No one anymore feels the presence of the Almighty. And why? Why?"

"Could we have this deep discussion another time?" said Agatha. "I want to find out who committed these murders and no one in this village seems to care."

"And just what do you think I was doing?" demanded Guy. "I was praying for help. I will let you know when I get an answer."

"How will you know it's not yourself talking to yourself?" asked Agatha. "I'm afraid these days that the police demand proof."

"Once I know who it is," said the vicar, "I will be pointed in the right direction. Now, if you will excuse me . . ."

"Come on, Roy," said Agatha, who had come to the conclusion that the vicar was bonkers.

They stood in the church porch. "Got your brolly?" asked Roy. "Hasn't it got dark?"

"That man is a bottle of communion wine short of a chalice," said Agatha. "Praying for an answer. I've never heard such a load of rubbish."

A jagged flash of lightning struck the ground in front of the porch and a great crack of thunder crashed about their ears.

"Yipes!" said Roy, clutching Agatha. "Maybe he got an answer."

"Or maybe I got an answer," said Agatha. "He's mad. I never noticed that before. Let's run before we get soaked."

But a curtain of rain was sweeping through the village and they had to go to their rooms in the inn and change into dry clothes.

By the time they met up again, the storm was rolling away to the east and a thin, pale sunlight was bathing the village. Water was dripping down from the thatched roofs.

"Now what?" asked Roy.

"I want to have a talk to Clarice, the vicar's wife."

"He scares me. What if he's there?"

"So what. He's just a religious nut."

They walked to the vicarage, Agatha striding ahead and Roy trailing reluctantly behind.

Toni had said a firm goodbye to her latest date the evening before. After James Lacey's company, the young man seemed shallow and boring. She had just finished with the latest find-out-if-my-husband-is-cheating-on-me case and she felt listless and lonely. She returned to the office and typed up her report. To her irritation, Simon was patiently waiting for her. "Fancy a meal?" he asked hopefully.

"No, I want an early night," said Toni.

Simon sadly watched her blond head as she bent over her computer keyboard before saying, "Goodnight."

Toni finished her report, but instead of going home, she got into her car and drove to Carsely. In Lilac Lane, she noticed with a sudden beating of her heart that James's car was parked outside his cottage. She parked her car and then tried to tell herself not to be silly.

James was inside, packing his suitcase. He felt ashamed of his treatment of Mary and knew he had raised hopes of marriage in her. As he earned most of his money by writing travel books, he had good excuse to get out of the village. He had naïvely tried to pretend that theirs was only a village friendship when he had seen her briefly in the village shop. When he had told her he was going on his travels, she had started to cry and had clutched hold of his sleeve as if to stop him leaving, watched by the curious eyes of some of the villagers.

"I feel like a cad," he said out loud. A sudden fear she might be lurking outside made him look out of his front window. He recognised Toni's little car. He flung open the door. "Toni!" he cried. "What are you doing here?"

Toni got out of her car, her face pink with embarrassment. "I had some financial reports for Agatha and I put them through her letterbox."

"I say, have you had dinner?"

"Not yet."

"I'm going off on my travels but I'd like something to eat first. Join me?"

"I'd love to."

Agatha and Roy were just approaching the vicarage when they met Clarice, who shied at the sight of them like a startled horse.

"Can't speak," she said. "Got to read to old Mrs. Tripp."

"I thought she was in hospital," said Agatha.

"Got out today and Guy insists I look after her."

"We'll do it," said Agatha, anxious to find out whether the old lady might have an idea of who it was had spiked her drink with laxative.

"Oh, would you? Thanks most awfully. She gives me the creeps."

"And may we call on you afterwards?"

"What? Oh, well, I suppose so. Who's this?"

"Sorry. Friend of mine, Roy Silver. Roy, Clarice Enderbury. See you later."

"So I get to see the horrible Mrs. Tripp," said Roy.

"We have to read to her first. Then with any luck we might get some information out of her."

They rang the bell at Mrs. Tripp's cottage and then they could hear her calling, "The door's open."

They went into her parlour, where the old lady sat, wrapped in a large grey shawl.

"Who's this?" demanded Mrs. Tripp, looking Roy up and down. "Toy boy?"

"A colleague of mine, Roy Silver."

"Don't look much like a detective to me," commented Mrs. Tripp. "Puff of wind would blow you away, young man."

"I'm ever so fearfully strong and I've a black belt in karate," lied Roy.

"Well, well, don't stand there. Read to me." She handed Agatha a copy of a book called *The Colours of White*. "Page ninety-two."

Agatha and Roy sat down and Agatha turned to page ninety-two. "He tied her to the bed," she began, "and he could feel the rousing of his passion. 'Slut!' he said and struck her across her face. 'I'm going to f . . .'"

Agatha stared at the old lady. "Do you enjoy this filth?"

"Great stuff," cackled Mrs. Tripp. "Read on."

"I would like to ask you a few questions," said Agatha.

"Read!"

Agatha decided maliciously to make it all up. "The door burst open and Jason Strongfellow erupted into the room. He felled Jasper with a single blow to the jaw and then released Felicity and gathered her trembling body in his strong arms."

"She's asleep," whispered Roy. "She's got some nice stuff here, but so many photographs."

"She was in service."

"So what do we do now?"

"We wait," said Agatha. "She'll wake up soon."

I'm not doing anything wrong, James Lacey told himself as he looked across the table in a Thai restaurant in

Evesham at Toni's glowing face. I'm only being a friend to her.

They were seated at a window table, and across the street, Carsely gossip Mrs. Arnold, who had followed them, studied their happy faces avidly. She drove back to her cottage and looked up Agatha's e-mail address and began to write.

"Why have you stopped reading?" demanded Mrs. Tripp suddenly.

"Been reading for ages," said Agatha. "Now, you must have an idea of who put that stuff in your drink. Who visited you that day?"

"There was Jenny Soper. She often shops for me. She came with that Peter Suncliff. Let me see. Henry Bruce came to unstop the sink. Vicar called round to say his wife would be coming to read to me. Ada White and her husband called with some scones."

Agatha groaned. "It seems as if one of an awful lot of people could have done it. Are you sure you don't know which one?"

"Nary a clue."

The old lady looked so complacent that Agatha said crossly, "Aren't you afraid?"

"When you get to my age, death ain't so scary. Besides, I had a good clean-out."

Roy suddenly said, "You know, I think you've got a good idea who is responsible. I think you must know an awful lot about everyone in this village."

"Oh, get out of here, you piece of piss," said Mrs. Tripp viciously. "Go on!"

Outside, Agatha asked Roy, "Why did you say that?"

"Just thought I would needle her and see what happened. I'm hungry."

"Let's go to the pub. I could do with a drink," said Agatha. "I hope they're still serving. It's pretty late."

Moses told them dinner was over but his wife could make them ham omelettes. Agatha went up to her room and brought down her laptop. "I'll just check if there are any urgent e-mails," she said, putting it on the table and switching it on.

"Too late. Here's our food," said Roy.

Agatha put her computer on the table next to them. They ate in silence, each immersed in their own thoughts. Roy was wondering if his trip was a waste of time. Nothing was happening, and nothing happening meant no press, and no press meant no publicity for himself.

Agatha found her thoughts turning to James Lacey. He was going to marry Mary Gotobed. Surely Toni was safe.

She moved to the next table and switched on her

computer. She scowled when she saw there was a letter from Mrs. Arnold. She clicked on it and read: "Dear Mrs. Raisin, I thought you ought to know that Mr. Lacey has cruelly spurned Mary Gotobed and turned his attentions to a girl young enough to be his grand-daughter, namely Toni Gilmour. They were lovey-dovey in a restaurant in Evesham this evening. It's disgraceful and ought to be stopped. Yrs. Rose Arnold."

"What's up?" asked Roy. "You look as if someone's poisoned you."

"It's James," said Agatha bleakly. "He's romancing Toni."

"Go on. He's always been like an uncle to her."

"What can I do?"

"Nothing," said Roy. "You've interfered in Toni's life before. She'd never forgive you and you'd lose a good detective. James is a sensible man."

"So I'm off on my travels," said James as he drove Toni back to Carsely to pick up her car.

"Where are you going?"

"Various places in Spain. I'm doing a budget holiday book and with the recession in Spain there are a lot of holiday bargains."

"Sounds great," said Toni wistfully. "I haven't had a holiday in ages."

"I say, why not come with me? I could cover your expenses."

"I've got holiday owing. But what would Agatha say?"

"Agatha needn't know."

"I'll phone her now. The work's just begun to slack off. I'll need to lie."

Toni arranged to meet James at Birmingham Airport on the following morning, where he would arrange a ticket for her. She said goodbye to him and then parked a little way up the road and called Agatha.

"This is very short notice," said Toni, "but a friend of mine has a villa in Bulgaria and I've got a chance of a free holiday. I'd like to go off tomorrow for two weeks. Work has gone slack so everything will be okay."

"Have you seen James?" asked Agatha.

"Yes," said Toni. "We had dinner and then he took off for the airport. He's been very kind to me. I'll miss his company."

"I'm surprised you have anything in common. He's so very much older than you."

"Well, he's always been like one of the family. I'll phone Mrs. Freedman tomorrow and bring her up to date. I really could do with a holiday."

"It's all very sudden. I'll go to the office myself tomorrow and allocate the work. Have a good time."

When Agatha rang off, she said to Roy, "Everything's okay. That was Toni. She's off to Bulgaria to stay at a friend's villa and James has gone off on his travels. She does seem to think of him as some sort of relative."

"And is James going to Bulgaria?"

"Oh, drop it, Roy. I've been worrying about nothing. I'm going up to the office tomorrow. Want to come?"

"I'll stay here. I might find out something."

Roy was a bit of a fantasist. When Agatha had left the following day, he dreamed of finding out the identity of the murderer and seeing his own photograph on the front page of all the newspapers. The more he thought about it, the surer he became that the vicar was the culprit. The man was obviously a religious maniac.

He decided to stalk Clarice and catch her on her own. Villagers looked at him curiously as he hung about the village street near the vicarage. A pretty, young woman who introduced herself as Jenny Soper at last accosted him and asked if she could help.

"I'm down here to help Agatha find the murderer," said Roy.

"And who does Mrs. Raisin think it is?"

"She hasn't a clue. But I know."

"Who is it?"

"I only need a little more proof. Wait and see."

Jenny went off to do her shopping at the village store. She was hailed by Peter Suncliff. "What's that odd young man doing hanging about?"

"He's convinced he knows the identity of the murderer."

The little shop was crowded. There was a startled silence.

Henry Bruce said, "Do you think he really knows something?"

"Not really," said Jenny. "I mean, he would have told that Raisin woman and she's gone off to London."

"Is anyone going to carry my groceries for me?" demanded Mrs. Tripp.

The villagers began to melt away. No one wanted to be trapped into reading to old Mrs. Tripp.

Clarice Enderbury had already done her shopping. She hurried out into the main street. Roy came rushing up to meet her. "I've been looking for you," he said.

"I'm busy," snapped Clarice. "What do you want?"

The villagers had crowded out of the shop behind Clarice, but stopped to listen.

"In my opinion, your husband is the murderer," said Roy.

Clarice's green eyes bored into him. "You will be hearing from our lawyers. I'll sue your socks off. That's slander. That's defamation of character."

"I said, 'In my opinion,'" panted Roy. "You can't sue me."

"Wait and see," said Clarice grimly.

Peter Suncliff strode forward. "Get out of our village, you little pipsqueak. We don't want you here."

Roy cringed as he looked from one angry face to the other. For a second, he seemed to see them dressed in seventeenth-century clothes and out on a witch hunt. He scampered off back to the inn.

He feverishly began to pack. He should never have come to this Cotswold version of *Brigadoon*.

He settled his bill and carried his suitcase out to the car. A thin ghostly mist had descended on the village. An old elm tree outside the pub was silhouetted against the mist, looking threatening, like a tree in a fairy story.

He threw his suitcase in the backseat and tried to start the car but the engine would not turn over. Roy phoned the Automobile Association, who said it would take an hour to get to him as they were very busy. He contemplated going back into the pub for lunch, but the villagers were filing in for the lunchtime session and he wanted to avoid another confrontation.

He locked the doors of his car and settled down to wait. He was bored. He remembered he had a flask of brandy in the glove compartment. One nip wouldn't put him over the limit. He fished out the flask and took a swig. Almost immediately, he felt a fiery pain in his throat and a wave of nausea racked his thin body. Outside, the elm tree seemed to have grown a face and was leering at him. He let out one terrified scream before he blacked out.

"There's that young man in his car," said Jenny as she and Peter were about to walk into the pub.

"Silly fool," said Peter. "I'm going to send him on his way." He peered in the window.

The mist shifted and a weak ray of sunshine fell on Roy's chalk-white face. Peter tugged at the door of the car but found it locked.

"He's had a seizure." He grabbed a rock from the inn courtyard, ran round to the passenger side and smashed the window. He unlocked the door.

"He's in such a bad way," he shouted to Jenny. "I don't know if it would even be safe to wait for an ambulance. Oh, there's that detective."

Bill Wong with Alice came driving up. They had come back to the village to question people again.

Peter quickly told Bill about the problem. They eased Roy out of his car. Bill administered CPR. Roy mumbled something but his pulse was weak. He was laid on the backseat of the unmarked police car. Bill bagged up Roy's flask and left Alice to guard Roy's car for any further evidence and then raced off in the direction of Mircester with the siren blaring.

Agatha was horrified when she received a call from Bill, asking if she knew any members of Roy's family. "His parents are dead and he hasn't any brothers or sisters," said Agatha. "What's happened?"

"He collapsed in his car in Piddlebury. There was a brandy flask on the seat beside him. It looked at first like a heart attack but a doctor at the hospital said he'd seen a case like this before and he's pretty sure it's digitalis poisoning. He extracted some spores from the back of his throat. He says it looks like foxglove. There's a lot of foxgloves in cottage gardens and people don't often know it is a very poisonous plant."

"Will he live?"

"Yes. He got the right treatment in time. If he hadn't been found right away, it could have been deadly."

"When can I see him?"

"Maybe tomorrow. Look, Agatha, what the hell is going on in that village? You're not keeping information back?"

"No. I can't get anywhere. It's an odd place. There are usually newcomers in Cotswold villages who would be happy to talk, but in that little place, they all close ranks. It's as if they would rather have a murderer in their midst than let in the outside world."

Agatha switched on her computer and logged into the cases her small staff were currently covering. Mrs. Freedman came back into the office, carrying a shopping bag, and shied guiltily as she saw Agatha.

"Just nipped out for a moment," she said.

"I've been here an hour," said Agatha severely.

"Well, I often work overtime. And my work is up to date."

Agatha told her about Roy. "Don't you think that's one case you should drop?" said Mrs. Freedman anxiously. "Don't you think you might be next?"

"I'll just watch what I drink," said Agatha. "New hairstyle?"

Mrs. Freedman patted a head of tight grey curls. "It's a new hairdresser. Ever so good, he is. Gives a really stiff perm."

Simon came in. "Oh, you're back," he said to Agatha. "I heard about Roy on the radio. Would you like me to go there instead of you?"

"No, I'll get back tomorrow after I've had a chance to see Roy. I'm surprised Toni left so abruptly."

"She's gone off with James Lacey," said Simon.

"But she said she was going to Bulgaria!" exclaimed Agatha.

Simon had no intention of telling Agatha that he had been stalking Toni, and that he had followed her to Birmingham Airport. "A friend of mine happened to be at Birmingham Airport. He had met Toni at one time when she was having a drink with me. He said she was lovey-dovey with some man old enough to be her father."

"It can't have been James," said Agatha.

"Tall, black hair going grey at the temples, handsome, six feet tall, blue eyes?"

Agatha slumped down in her chair. "What can we do? This is a disaster. I'll phone Toni on her mobile." Agatha waited anxiously but Toni's phone went straight to the messaging service. Agatha rang off. "I can't nag her. It's her life."

James may have been Agatha's ex-husband, but she felt he was *her* James. Part of her missed her old obsession with him. In fact, Agatha without any obsession to colour her days often felt at a loss.

Her phone rang. It was Charles Fraith. "What's all this about Roy?" he asked.

"The village murderer appears to have tried to poison him," said Agatha. "I must see you, Charles. Where are you?"

"I'm in Mircester."

"Meet me in the bar of the George. I need your help."

"You look almost feverish," commented Charles. "Gin and tonic?"

"Please."

"Now, this business of Roy is very scary," said Charles.

"There's something worse than that."

"Can't imagine. What?"

"Toni's gone off on holiday with James."

"Ah."

"Is that all you have to say?"

"Calm down. I saw James briefly some days before he left. He was planning to go to Spain to write a travel book on budget accommodation. It's not like five-star hotel accommodation where a man of James's years with a young blonde would pretty much pass unnoticed. He's going to have to put up with people thinking she's his daughter."

"What came over him? He's usually so sensible. First he's going to marry the village frump, then he dumps her—and that's right out of character—and then he falls for Toni. We must do something."

"No, Agatha. Leave them alone and they'll come home, wagging their tails behind them. And keep your mouth shut when they do come back. I'll bet anything,

Toni will be feeling silly and James will be feeling like an idiot and the last thing they'll need is you jumping all over their feelings. Now, let's go and see Roy."

"Bill said I could see him tomorrow."

"Not like you to obey orders. Drink up!"

"Should we buy white coats and pretend to be doctors?" asked Agatha as Charles parked outside the hospital.

"No, it's the visiting hour."

"He'll have a police guard."

"So? We're his uncle and aunt. This James business is fogging your brain."

"But Bill will find out and he'll be furious."

"Oh, I'll think of something. He's probably still in intensive care. Let's make our way there."

Agatha hated hospitals with their long corridors and their smells of disinfectant.

"That must be where he is," said Charles, stopping suddenly and pointing to where a policeman sat on a chair outside a room. "I think we need to get rid of him. Let's retreat round the corner."

"There are CCTV cameras all over the place," said Agatha. "I'm going to try the direct approach." Followed by Charles, she marched up to the policeman.

She held out her business card. "I am Agatha Raisin,

Mr. Silver's friend, and this is Sir Charles Fraith. He has no relatives. We would like to check on his condition."

"I'm not to let anyone in who isn't hospital staff or police," said the officer. "But I can tell you, he's recovered consciousness."

"Then ask him if he wants to see us," said Agatha. "It is the visiting hour."

"I'll need to phone for permission." The policeman walked a little way away from them, turned his back, and took out his phone.

Agatha, followed by Charles, walked straight into the room. Roy was propped up against pillows, speaking into his phone. "Yes, that's me. Roy Silver. What? No, I'm not afraid. I'm used to danger. I have solved cases for Agatha Raisin before."

Agatha coughed loudly and Roy gave a squawk of alarm and rang off.

"You're well enough to phone the press, I see," said Agatha. "Quick! What happened?"

Roy had just finished telling them about the brandy flask and that it had been discovered that his car engine had been disabled when the policeman came into the room and ordered them out. "Did you see anyone?" said Agatha, as they were hustled to the door.

"No one," said Roy. "But that vicar's wife's got it in for me."

"Out!" shouted the policeman.

"I'd better get back to that wretched village," said Agatha.

"I'll follow you down," said Charles.

Agatha gave him a gruff thanks, to hide the fact that she was relieved not to be going to Piddlebury on her own. "I think I'll drop over to Carsely first and see how my cats are getting on and maybe visit Mrs. Bloxby."

"Then I'll see you down there," said Charles. "I'll drop you back at your car."

Doris Simpson was busy cleaning Agatha's cottage. Agatha's cats were playing with Doris's cat, Scrabble, in the garden and seemed indifferent to Agatha's arrival.

"I should have got a dog," said Agatha huffily. "Dogs are affectionate."

"You don't want one o' them," said Doris. "Like children, they are. Now, cats are independent and can look after themselves. Did you hear about Mr. Lacey breaking Mary Gotobed's heart?"

"Yes. Very unlike him."

"Well, Mary's got herself engaged."

"To James?"

"No, to Tom Sodbury, him what has the farm over near Ebrington."

"That was quick work."

"Mary's been married twice before."

"How does she do it?"

Doris wiped the kitchen table. "Seems to me there's some women who are just the marrying kind."

Agatha paid her and then went up to the vicarage where she received a warm welcome from Mrs. Bloxby.

"Have you heard the news about Mary Gotobed?" asked Agatha.

"Yes, indeed. But hardly surprising."

"Why is that?"

"I always found her manipulative and sly. Mr. Lacey had a good escape."

Agatha's face darkened. "The silly idiot's got a crush on Toni and they've gone off on holiday together."

"Oh, well, that won't last."

"Why do you say that?"

"Because Mr. Lacey is a proud man. People will assume Toni is his daughter. He won't like that one bit."

"But what about Toni? I don't want her getting hurt."

"Oh, I should think she will find that Mr. Lacey abroad is not quite what she expected."

Toni had forgotten that James was investigating budget holidays and had imagined herself lazily sipping a long cold drink beside a swimming pool. But she found herself in a small hotel in a back street off the Ramblas in Barcelona. It was clean but very basic, a family hotel, where the owner welcomed James and "his daughter." James had said acidly that Toni was not his daughter whereupon the owner had a hurried consultation with his wife before allocating them their rooms.

But James had been embarrassed. On the first day, he told Toni that he would be investigating other budget hotels and suggested she went sightseeing on her own. Toni made her way to the Ramblas, Barcelona's famous main street. It started to rain so she went into a café, ordered a coffee, and looked bleakly around her. What had gone wrong? They had gone out for dinner the previous evening. James had been courteous and polite, but distant, as if he were entertaining a young relative with whom he had little in common.

Then, at breakfast, he had immersed himself behind a Spanish newspaper. Toni felt her temper beginning to rise. James was in a huff because the proprietor had thought she was James's daughter. What else was the man supposed to think, thought Toni, and then realised that they would probably get the same treatment in every hotel they went to and James would get gloomier and more embarrassed. It had all been one awful mistake.

The café was filling up. A girl of about her own age asked if she could share her table and Toni nodded.

Toni realised the girl had spoken English. "Are you here on holiday?" she asked.

"Yes, but my family live in Madrid."

"You're Spanish! Your English is excellent."

"I was educated in England. Are you enjoying yourself? My name is Marie."

"I'm Toni." Toni surveyed her new companion. Marie had large brown eyes and long black hair. She was wearing a flower-patterned short sheath dress and flat sandals. "And no, I am not enjoying myself."

"Is it because of the rain? Look! The sun is beginning to come out."

Toni had a sudden desire to confide in her and found herself telling Marie about James.

"That will not do at all," said Marie seriously. "Say you are married. Do you want your children to grow up with an old man?"

"I don't know what happened," said Toni miserably. "We had such fun. Now, he's as cold as ice."

"He has the decency to see it will not work. My family has an apartment here. I am staying with my sister. Join us for a few days."

"But what will I tell James?"

"The truth. I will collect you this evening. Give me the name of your hotel."

Toni wrote it down. "He cannot think highly of you to choose such a place."

"He's a travel writer. He's writing about budget holidays."

"I will call this evening. In the meantime, we will go to your hotel and collect your case and get you installed."

James, returning that evening, was handed a note by the owner. He read, "Dear James, It really is not working out and I am going to stay with a friend. I will call this evening at eight o'clock to explain things. Toni."

James felt he would give anything not to face Toni. He felt he must have run mad. But duty dictated that he was obliged to see this friend and make sure Toni was going to be all right.

He was sitting at the table outside the small hotel when he saw Toni approaching with another girl.

Toni introduced her new friend. She explained how they had met. "You see, James, it would be a better arrangement," said Toni. "I am going to stay with Marie for a week and then I will change my air ticket and leave for England."

"I am really very sorry," said James. "I had forgotten about the vast age difference. Please don't tell Agatha."

Chapter Six

Charles had just gone over Agatha's notes. "There's one person you seem to be forgetting," he said.

"Who's that?"

"Brian Summer."

"But he was cleared of the drug charge!"

"He's weird," said Charles. "Why stay on in this village? He says the police questioning upset him and he had to take time off. So why not clear off to somewhere where the police aren't questioning? Then there's Ada White. It was her elderberry wine that did the damage. Can she really be innocent?"

"She wasn't anywhere near Gloria's at the time of the murder."

"You forget. No one had to be near Gloria's. All anyone had to do was nip in the back door and leave that bottle in the cellar. All these alibis aren't worth a damn."

"I think the bottle was placed there that morning. The murderer couldn't risk Gloria offering a drink to, say, the vicar, and the wrong person being poisoned. Also, you've forgotten. The bottle and glass were taken away."

"Have it your way. But let's see Brian Summer."

Ada said Brian was out walking in the woods. "He's very fragile," she said defensively. "Don't you go upsetting him."

"Whereabouts in the woods?" asked Charles.

"I don't know. I don't go persecuting him."

"The woods aren't large," said Agatha as they set out. Sunlight was shining in slants through the old trees. It was very quiet. Not a bird was singing. They wandered on, looking to right and left.

At last they reached the glade where Agatha had found Brian the last time she had hunted him, but the glade was empty.

"This is odd," said Charles, bending over a flat stone under an old oak tree. "Come and look at this, Aggie."

"Don't call me Aggie. What is it?"

"That looks like dried blood."

The stone was a square slab of limestone. Agatha bent down and peered at the dark splashes on it.

"I think it's some sort of altar," said Charles. "Do they practise witchcraft in these parts?"

"Wouldn't surprise me," said Agatha gloomily. "There are still covens in the Cotswolds. I remember a case before. They actually advertise forthcoming events in some magazine. Pretty harmless."

"Not if they're sacrificing something. There's a full moon tonight," said Charles. "Might be worth staying up tonight in the woods."

"And if nothing happens?"

"We can make mad, passionate love under the trees."

"I didn't think you did love," said Agatha acidly. "I only thought you did sex."

"Naughty. Look! I think there's someone over there."

Charles ran off and Agatha stumbled after him, caught her foot in a tree root and fell flat.

When she got up, Charles was coming back to join her. "It was Summer," he said. "He took off at a great pace when he saw me. Now what? Do we go back to the farmhouse and see if he turns up?"

"Let's go and see Jerry Tarrant, the head of the parish council. I want to know more about this secretive little village. The reason we can't get a lead on anything is because I feel everyone is ganging up on us."

Jerry Tarrant was so neat and barbered, and with the knife-edged crease in his jeans and his highly polished shoes, he made the immaculate Charles Fraith look almost casual.

"Is there witchcraft practised in this village?" demanded Agatha.

"Not since the eighteenth century," said Jerry. "What makes you ask?"

"We were up in the glade in the woods and there was a stone like an altar and it had dried blood on it."

"Oh, that stone. Maybe children."

"That's an odd thing," commented Charles. "I haven't seen any children in this village."

"We have some during the holidays. Ada White's grandchildren were here on a visit."

"Before or after the murders?"

"Before."

"It's been raining since," said Charles.

"I can't think of any reason. Perhaps someone tripped over it."

"I'm doing my best," said Agatha, exasperated. "But the village seems to be closing ranks against me."

"Well, they do seem to cling to the idea that the murders must have been committed by some outsider."

"What outsider would know that the back door of Gloria's cottage was usually open? What outsider would have any reason for such an elaborate murder? And for what reason would an outsider hang around to try to murder me?"

Jerry Tarrant clasped his well-manicured hands together. He did not look at them but addressed his remarks to the head of a stuffed fox on the wall to his left.

"I really think you should just leave things alone, Mrs. Raisin."

"You want me to stop working?"

Jerry stared at the fox, which looked glassily back.

"I think it would be best. I do not have unlimited funds. The murders were unfortunate . . ."

"Unfortunate!" howled Agatha.

". . . but I feel if you stopped interrogating people, then the village would settle down again."

"The whole idea of me being employed," said Agatha, "was to stop the bad feeling in the village, everyone suspecting everyone else."

"But that was early days. The consensus of opinion is that it was some madman who happened to be passing through."

"Stop looking at that damned fox and look at me," said Charles. "You're frightened. Who frightened you?"

"No one. Please leave. Send me your bill. I am sorry I cannot be of further help."

Agatha stood up and leaned over the desk, her bear-like eyes boring into him. "I will not be defeated. I will stay until I've got to the bottom of this."

Jerry sat with his head bowed while they left.

Outside, Agatha said to Charles, "Are you sure he was frightened?"

"Yes. He was sweating. I could smell him."

"I couldn't smell anything."

"You smoke."

"So do you!"

"Not as much as you."

"Talking about cigarettes, I need another packet," said Agatha. "Let's drop into the village shop."

The woman behind the counter shook her head when she heard Agatha's request. "Don't have no cigarettes no more," she said.

"Look, as you know, I am Agatha Raisin, I am a detective and I know you keep the cigarettes in the cupboards under the counter."

"Don't no more," said the woman stubbornly. She

had a thin, wrinkled face with a large nose shadowing a small pursed mouth.

"Here! What you doing?" she yelled, because Agatha had darted around the counter, opened a cupboard and selected a packet of cigarettes. She took out her purse, found the exact money and slammed it on the counter.

As she and Charles turned away, the woman shouted, "Get out of our village. No one wants you here!"

"This is mediaeval," said Agatha. "They'll be stoning us next." She stopped short in the entrance to the Green Man. Their suitcases were packed and standing in the hall. Agatha stormed into the bar. "What is the meaning of this?" she demanded. "How dare you pack our things without our permission?"

"It's like this," said Moses awkwardly. "My trade depends on the villagers and they say unless you leave, they're not going to come here anymore."

"It's against the law!" howled Agatha.

Moses leaned on the bar and looked at them sadly. "This is my place and if I say you've got to go, then that's it."

"Come on, Agatha," said Charles. "Let's get out of here. Get back to your office and study your notes in peace."

Agatha reluctantly left with him. As they stood by

their respective cars, Charles said, "I'll call on you in the next week or so and see how you are getting on."

Feeling bewildered and defeated, Agatha drove off. She suddenly remembered the idea of witchcraft, but the thought of hiding in the woods on her own no longer seemed like such a good idea.

In the month that followed, an unexpected rush of work kept Agatha and her staff busy. Toni was quiet and subdued. Agatha longed to ask her what had happened but felt sure Toni would be furious with her and besides, she had promised herself she would not interfere in the girl's private life again. Roy, fully recovered, was back at work. Charles had not called and Agatha felt hurt, despite the fact that he had a habit of disappearing from her life for long periods at a time.

Agatha felt that when things died down, she would somehow find a way to return to Piddlebury. She did not like the feeling of being defeated.

Then one morning, she received a letter from a firm of lawyers, Desy, Swinge and Tollent, in Oxford. It said she should call on them to learn something of interest to her.

She drove immediately to Oxford and to the lawyers' offices on Beaumont Street. A secretary offered her coffee and said Mr. Swinge would only be a few moments.

Pale sunlight flooded the Dickensian premises where the only modern thing seemed to be the blond secretary. Behind her rose boxes and boxes of files to the high Georgian ceiling.

The phone on her desk rang. She answered it and then stood up. "Mr. Swinge will see you now."

She pushed open the door to an inner office and ushered Agatha in. Mr. Swinge was a small round fat youngish man with a broad smile creasing his cheeks.

"Please sit down, Mrs. Raisin," he said. "You were working this year for a Mr. Jeremy Tarrant of Piddlebury?"

"Yes, what's happened to him?"

"He died two weeks ago."

"I never heard a thing about it!" exclaimed Agatha. "Was he murdered?"

"No, no. A heart attack. I have a letter here he lodged with us just before his death, to be opened on his death. In it he writes that he wishes the sum of five thousand pounds to be paid out of his estate to Mrs. Agatha Raisin of the Agatha Raisin agency in Mircester so that she may use the funds to continue her investigations into the murders in Piddlebury."

"He must have expected something to happen to him," said Agatha. "Was there a police investigation?"

"Yes, there was an autopsy. It was, indeed, a heart attack."

"Who is the main beneficiary?"

"I don't know that I should . . ."

"My dear man, if he wants me to solve those murders, I need to know as much as possible."

"He had no relatives. He was an adopted child. His adopted parents were wealthy manufacturers of tourist souvenirs. On their death, they left their fortune to Mr. Tarrant. The bulk of his estate, apart from twenty thousand pounds to the church in Piddlebury and his bequest to you, goes to the Animal Rescue Park in Mircester. I can give you a cheque now."

Agatha hesitated. This was one case that she would have dearly loved to abandon. She cringed at the idea of going back to that odd and sinister village. But Agatha's whole belligerent life had been filled with facing up to small and large fears.

"I'll take the cheque. But I am going to begin by investigating the death of Jerry Tarrant!"

On her return to Mircester, late in the day, Agatha asked Toni to join her for dinner. "I've got something to discuss with you," said Agatha.

I may as well get it over with, thought Toni. I've known by her manner that she wants to ask me about James.

But when they were seated in the dining room of

the George, Agatha surprised Toni by telling her about Jerry's bequest and ended by saying, "I don't know where to start. If I try to book into the pub, Moses will refuse to have me."

"There are surely villages nearby," said Toni. "You could stay in one of those. And you might get some gossip about Piddlebury."

"Good idea. I've got Patrick trying to find out more about Jerry Tarrant's death."

"You think it was murder?"

"It does seem strange. Roy was nearly killed with a dose of digitalis. If the same thing happened to Jerry, then it might look just like a heart attack. I think you should come with me . . . unless it interferes with your social life."

"You want to ask me about James," said Toni.

"Not any of my business," said Agatha.

"No, it isn't. But I'd like to clear the air before we start working together. I am always attracted to older men. James seemed such fun and we had a good time together. Somehow, it all seemed so innocent. I went to Barcelona with him. He was going to write about budget hotels so we ended up in one where the owner thought I was James's daughter. That hurt his pride. He went all cold and formal. I met this girl in a café and we became friends and I moved into her apartment. End of story."

"Oh, well," said Agatha. "You'd be better off with someone of your own age. Simon seems pretty keen."

"I think Simon is stalking me and that's just not healthy. I've given up looking. Can we talk about something else?"

"Sure. I've got some ordnance survey maps here. Now, about twelve miles from Piddlebury, there's a village called Under Pleasance."

"I'll check it on my phone for a hotel or an inn," said Toni.

"Better order our food first," said Agatha, indicating the hovering waiter.

Neither felt like being adventurous so they both ordered steaks and chips and a bottle of Merlot.

Toni took out her phone. "There is an inn at Under Pleasance," she said. "There's nothing about rooms. I'll phone them up."

As Toni phoned and found out that she could book two rooms, Agatha covertly studied the girl. Toni's fair skin was lightly tanned and she always seemed to carry a glowing aura of good health. How could any man resist that, thought Agatha sourly. When she had been Toni's age, she remembered having a lumpy figure and a spotty face from bad eating habits.

"When do we start?" asked Toni.

"We'll meet up at the office at nine o'clock tomorrow

morning," said Agatha. "You take your car as well in case we have to split up for any reason. It's Saturday tomorrow, but you can claim the overtime."

Agatha went back to her cottage after dinner. She looked at James's cottage before she let herself in but it was dark and silent. She noticed his thatch was in need of repair—an expensive job. Perhaps she might get it done for him for Christmas. Perhaps he might smile at her and say, "You are the only woman in my life, Agatha." Perhaps . . . She gave herself a shake. All that obsession had gone.

She got a rare welcome from her cats. Before she drifted off to sleep that night, she had a sudden sharp desire to leave the whole horrible case alone. Piddlebury frightened her, but that was something Agatha would not admit to herself.

With Toni leading the way and Agatha following, they arrived the next morning at the village of Under Pleasance. It was quite a large, prosperous-looking village, a mixture of old and new buildings. The inn was called the Jolly Farmer. A painting of an old-fashioned farmer with a rubicund face and wearing a white smock hung over the low door, surrounded by late-flowering rambling roses. The day was sunny and there was an autumnal smell of bonfires in the air.

The inn was well-appointed, and, as Toni had discovered, fairly expensive. It even boasted a receptionist who showed them to their rooms. Agatha's room had a four-poster, and gaily coloured chintz curtains at the latticed window. On a table by the window was a presentation bowl of fruit and a bottle of wine. Agatha's spirits rose. The very comfort of the place seemed to restore her confidence in her detective abilities.

She unpacked and knocked at Toni's door. When Toni answered, Agatha said, "I'll be downstairs in the bar."

The bar was low and beamed and decorated with hunting scenes. Only a few people were in the bar, but they smiled and said, "Good morning" when Agatha entered. Agatha ordered a gin and tonic and then took her glass out to a bench outside the inn and lit a cigarette.

It was peaceful. Two women rode past, the sunlight gleaming on the flanks of their well-groomed-looking horses. The houses on either side of the village street had expensive cars parked outside. The street opened out onto a village green with a duck pond and then continued on the other side. Agatha, leaning forward, could just see a general store by the pond.

Toni joined her, carrying a glass of lager. "This is a great place," said Toni. "Have you seen the menu?"

Agatha shook her head.

"Good English food," said Toni. "Steak and kidney pie, rack of lamb, things like that."

"Do they have any salads?" asked Agatha. "I'm on a diet."

"I think so. What a lovely place. Makes me wish we were on holiday. Where do we start? Oh, I looked through the notes again last night. There's a full moon tonight. We could go over to the Piddlebury Woods and see if there is any sign of witchcraft."

"We could do that," said Agatha reluctantly. "I suppose if they're crazy enough to practise witchcraft, then they might all be in on the murders. I can't imagine why Gloria was murdered. I mean she took things and didn't give them back. Hardly a fault to promote murder."

"The people who own this inn took it over six months ago," said Toni. "I found that out from the barman. So they may not know much about Piddlebury. Where should we start? Do you think there's some vicar's wife like Mrs. Bloxby?"

"Mrs. Bloxby is a one-off," said Agatha. "Still, is there a church here? I can't see one."

"It's just out of sight behind the houses on the green," said Toni. "I asked. There's also a petrol station, just outside the village on the other side."

"How does a petrol station help?"

"Was there one in Piddlebury?"

"No."

"So maybe the villagers get their petrol here. There must have been a lot of gossip over the murders."

My brain seems to have stopped working, thought Agatha, suddenly feeling outclassed by her young assistant.

She looked at her watch. "Let's have lunch first."

Lunch was a mistake, thought Agatha, as an hour and a half later, they walked along the village street. Why on earth had she eaten stuffed garlic mushrooms, followed by steak and kidney pie and ending up with a large portion of icky-sticky pudding? She could feel the waistband of her skirt uncomfortably tight. Toni, in a blue cotton sheath dress and flat sandals, looked as slim as ever.

The sun was quite warm and there was a lazy, rich feel about the place. It was quite near the Oxford motorway, which explained the open feel of the place compared to Piddlebury.

"Do you want to start questioning people in the shop?" asked Toni.

"I don't want to alert a lot of people as to why we're here at the moment," said Agatha. "We'll start with the vicarage."

The vicarage was a large, rather ugly Victorian building next to an old church with a squat Norman tower.

A brick path divided two small patches of lawn. The only flowers were two pots of geraniums on either side of the door. Toni rang the bell.

The door was flung open by a large muscular woman wearing a faded housedress.

"Yes?" she demanded.

"I am Agatha Raisin, a private detective," said Agatha, "and I am investigating the murders at Piddlebury."

"So what's that got to do with me?" She had a large round head topped with unruly wisps of grey hair and her small mouth was pursed in disapproval. Then she suddenly smiled. "You're that woman with the omelette on her head. Best laugh I've had in ages. Come in."

For once, Agatha was glad of that clowning episode on television.

The woman led the way into a gleaming modern kitchen. Agatha reflected that the vicar must have private means.

"I am Margaret Swithin," said the vicar's wife, sitting down at a kitchen table and indicating that they should do the same. "Was that a real omelette?"

"Yes," said Agatha, trying to smile and failing miserably. "Look, these murders . . ."

"And is this your daughter?"

"Sorry, I forgot to introduce her. My assistant, Toni Gilmour. Now, about Piddlebury?"

"Never go near the place. My husband, Colin, now, he has to preach at several churches around here, but not Piddlebury."

"But didn't the murders cause a lot of gossip in this village?"

"Of course! Some of them went over to rubberneck. So vulgar. I mean, nothing to do with us."

"I think I would like to meet one of these vulgar people," said Agatha.

"Don't tell her I gave you her name! She's Dorothy Callant. Widow. Lives at Rose Cottage on the green. Worst gossip I ever came across."

Dorothy Callant, a small sixtyish woman with a shock of dyed red hair and a withered face, declared she was delighted to meet them. When Agatha said she wanted to find out as much as she could about Piddlebury, Dorothy ushered them into a cluttered parlour, exclaiming as she swept newspapers and film magazines off chairs and dumped them on the floor, "How exciting! I watch *Miss Marple* on television. That series must be a help to you, dear."

"It's fiction," said Agatha patiently.

"But her age! People must be surprised to see someone of your age, dear, acting as a detective."

"Mrs. Raisin has many years to go before she reaches anything like Miss Marple's age," said Toni.

"Really? Well, my eyesight is bad. Do sit down. May I offer you something?"

"No, thank you," said Agatha. "We've just had lunch. Did you visit Piddlebury?"

"Oh, yes. After the first murder, I drove over and called at the vicarage. But Mrs. Enderbury was quite rude. She even told me to push off! Not a lady, if you ask me. Ladies do not tell ladies to push off. I remember . . ."

"Let's keep to Piddlebury," said Agatha. "Talk to anyone else?"

"Yes, I talked to some people in the village shop. At first they were friendly, and then someone walked in and whispered something, and they all became quite hostile and told me if I didn't want to buy anything, to get out."

"Who was it who turned them against you?"

"Some woman called Sam. I mean, when women start using men's names, it shows they can't be very *nice* people, the sort of women who *compete* with men, which is folly, because the gentlemen *always* know better."

"How true," said Toni, much to Agatha's amazement. "Is there one particular gentleman whose advice you rely on?"

"Yes, indeed. Mr. Albert Earle, next door. So wise! 'Let it alone, Dorothy,' he said to me. 'Let the police do their work.' But he did take a run over there to see for himself."

"When was that?" asked Toni.

"It would be after that poor poacher was found poisoned. He said the villagers all told him that it must have been some maniac from outside. He told me that must be the case. Such a wise man!"

"Perhaps we had better speak to him," said Agatha.

"I'll come with you. Wait till I get my hat. This sun is so very bad for the complexion."

They followed her into a small hall where she took down a large straw hat from a hook and clamped it on her head.

Albert Earle was a small stocky man in his sixties. When he heard the reason for their visit, he stood aside and ushered Toni and Agatha in and then barred the way to Dorothy. "Leave this to me," he said. "I'll talk to you later," and he shut the door in Dorothy's face.

They could hear Dorothy on the other side of the door, making faint twittering noises of distress, like a dying bird.

"Come into the garden," said Albert. "It's too good a day to sit indoors."

Four chairs were arranged around an iron table on a small patio. The garden was ablaze with late roses and hollyhocks.

Toni thought that Albert needed a sun hat as much as the spurned Dorothy. His scalp showed scarlet under the thin wisps of hair combed over it and his face was fiery red as well.

He fixed the small watery eyes of the habitual drinker on Agatha and said pompously, "How can I be of assistance?"

"Piddlebury is an odd village," said Agatha. "The villagers appear to have closed ranks against outsiders. It's hard to get any information."

"They're an odd lot," said Albert. "I am on the parish council here and people respect me. But in Piddlebury, I was rather rudely told to mind my own business."

Agatha repressed a sigh. Albert was the sort of man that a lot of people, outside Piddlebury and in, would enjoy telling to mind his own business. He exuded pomposity from every pore.

"But if you are going back there," he said, "I will accompany you. Ladies should not go to such a dangerous place on their own."

"We're fine," said Agatha, rising to leave. "We're used to danger."

"That's the problem with you modern women," he said huffily. "Always going about getting raped and murdered because you wouldn't listen to sensible advice from some man."

"Well, it's usually some man who rapes," retorted Agatha. "Come along, Toni."

Outside, they decided to split up and knock on doors and try to find someone who knew something. No use keeping their visit secret anymore. Besides, Dorothy, the village gossip, had probably phoned up several people already. They arranged to meet in the pub that evening.

But it was a tired and defeated pair who finally met in the bar of the Jolly Farmer to compare notes.

Few of the people they had interviewed had visited Piddlebury. Those that had confessed they had gone out of curiosity, mostly visiting the village shop, but not one had anything interesting to say.

"We'll have some sleep after dinner and get over to that damned village for midnight," said Agatha.

Wearing dark clothes, they set out at half past eleven for Piddlebury. Agatha parked at the edge of the woods, farthest away from the village.

"Do you think you'll be able to find this glade with the altar stone in the darkness?" asked Toni.

"It's somewhere in the middle. Bound to find it," said Agatha hopefully.

They walked on through the silent wood. The branches of the trees met above them, cutting out the light from the moon. "I'm going to risk using a torch," said Agatha.

At last, after twenty minutes, Agatha whispered, "This is hopeless."

"Shh!" hissed Toni.

"What?"

"Listen!"

Agatha strained her ears. She could hear the faint sound of chanting.

"It's coming from over that direction," said Toni.

They made their way cautiously, hearing the weird voice getting louder, and then stopped suddenly when they found themselves on the edge of the glade, which was flooded with silver moonlight.

Brian Summer stood by the altar, a struggling hen in one hand. In the other, he held an open cutthroat razor.

Agatha Raisin had never considered herself particularly sentimental about birds and animals, but the sight of that hen was too much for her.

She strode into the clearing, shouting, "Leave that bird alone, you nut case!"

"Get away!" yelled Brian. "I must make this sacrifice."

As Agatha approached him, he waved the razor at her, shouting, "Get back!"

The bird struggled and gave a screech like a rusty gate.

Agatha slammed her torch hard down on his wrist, the one holding the bird. He screamed in pain and dropped the hen, which flapped off into the trees. Agatha backed off as he brandished the razor in her face.

Then his eyes seemed to roll back in his head and he fell to the ground, his feet hammering against the turf.

"He's having some sort of epileptic fit," said Toni. "Lay him on his side and make sure he doesn't swallow his tongue."

"You do it," said Agatha shakily. "I'm phoning for help."

It took half an hour for help to arrive and by that time Brian's fit was over but he was unconscious. Moses Green arrived in the glade, leading the police and an ambulance.

Brian was borne off and after preliminary questioning by police and then by Inspector Wilkes and a detective Agatha did not know, they were told to go immediately to police headquarters in Mircester.

When Agatha and Toni were waiting in reception to be interviewed again, Ada White arrived. "Is this your fault?" she demanded, glaring at Agatha.

"Brian Summer was in the glade in the woods with a razor about to sacrifice one of your hens," said Agatha.

"He what?"

Agatha patiently repeated what she had said. Ada looked shocked. "I've recently lost two geese and three hens. If this is true, he can pack his bags and leave. Oh, dear, he seemed such a nice quiet man."

Agatha was tired of being questioned. She had been taken to one of the newly refurbished interview rooms, boasting deep armchairs, and had to fight against falling asleep. When it was at last over and she signed a statement, she said, "About Jerry Tarrant's death. Did you ever think someone might have given him a shot of digitalis so that it would look like a heart attack?"

"An autopsy was carried out," said Wilkes, gathering up his notes and getting to his feet.

"And what was the result of the tox examination?" asked Agatha.

Wilkes stared at the desk. Then he said curtly, "I forget."

"No you don't," said Agatha with one of her flashes of intuition. "One wasn't carried out."

"There appeared to be no need for it," said Wilkes. "Several of the villagers confirmed that Mr. Tarrant had a weak heart."

Agatha gave a contemptuous snort. "And you believed them?"

"Mrs. Raisin, this interview is over. I would like to remind you for the hundredth time not to interfere in a police investigation."

Back at their inn, Agatha said to Toni, "We'll get some sleep and then I'm going over to see Ada White."

Toni hesitated in the doorway of her room. "I wonder if someone in Piddlebury is blackmailing people into silence. I mean, you said Jerry was frightened, and yet he cancelled your services. Then he leaves a will wanting you to carry on."

Agatha longed to contradict her out of petty jealousy. She thought the gods had given Toni enough gifts in a beautiful appearance without also endowing her with a sharp brain. But Agatha forced herself to say gruffly, "Good idea. We'll work on it tomorrow."

They drove towards Piddlebury on a perfect Indian summer's day. The fields were golden with stubble and cottage gardens ablaze with roses. They drove down deep lanes where trees arched over the road to form green tunnels, and then out into the mellow sunshine again. It was like driving through a series of English landscape paintings.

Agatha stopped just outside the village. She phoned Patrick. "See if you can find out from your police contacts if Brian Summer gives any reason for his odd behaviour. Who was he sacrificing poultry to? Or has his brain just snapped altogether?"

Patrick said he would look into it. Agatha reluctantly drove into the village. "We'll start with Clarice, the vicar's wife."

"Why? I thought we were going to see Ada White."

"Later. Clarice is in the best position to find out secrets that the villagers might not want exposed. From the smells of incense in the church, it means her husband is High Church of England and that can mean he takes confessions."

"Isn't there such a thing as the secrets of the confessional?" asked Toni.

"He might have blabbed to his wife. Here goes."

When Agatha and Toni got out of Agatha's car outside the vicarage, Agatha turned and looked down the main street. There was the faint noise of a hay baler up on the hill above the village, someone's television was playing, otherwise it was still and quiet. And yet Agatha could swear she felt menace emanating from somewhere. She shrugged off the feeling, and, followed by Toni, went up to the vicarage door and rang the bell.

The door was answered by the vicar, Guy Enderbury. He scowled down at them from his greater height. "Yes?"

"Has God told you who the murderer is?" asked Agatha.

"Not yet. I am still working on it," he said mildly. "Now, if you will excuse me . . ."

"We actually called to speak to your wife."

"If you go round the side of the vicarage, you will find her in the garden. My wife is a devoted gardener."

They followed the path around the side of the house. The "devoted gardener" was lying on a sun lounger, a cigarette in one hand and a book in the other.

She blinked up at them as they stood over her. "I thought you had got the message and decided to leave us alone," said Clarice. She swung her bare legs over the sun lounger and struggled to her feet.

"Is someone blackmailing you?" asked Agatha bluntly.

Clarice sat down again suddenly on the edge of the

lounger. "What a ridiculous idea," she said faintly. "I haven't any money. I do wish there was something exciting enough about me to prompt someone to want to blackmail me. Now, just go away."

"Blackmailers never give up," said Toni. "At first, you might have been blackmailed into silence, but they always come back for more."

"Listen to me, you amateur freaks. If anyone was blackmailing me, I'd tell the police. Now, you are trespassing. Go! Or do I have to call the police?"

Her green eyes suddenly glittered with tears.

Outside, Agatha said, "She was frightened. I swear we frightened her. Let's get to Ada's farm."

But as they approached Ada's farm, they could see police cars parked outside. "We'd better leave it until later," said Agatha.

They drove back into the village. Agatha called Patrick and asked if he had any news. Patrick said, "Brian Summer was sent an old book. He is subject to epileptic fits. The book was about old country remedies. Sort of white witchcraft. In it, the sufferer of epilepsy is told to sacrifice a bird at the full moon."

"How does a schoolteacher believe such tripe?"

"A schoolteacher with a belly full of magic mushrooms. Mrs. White said he had the use of a shed as a workshop. It was full of the things. She says she never went in there."

"Who sent him the book?" asked Agatha.

"Mrs. White doesn't know. She said it arrived for him in the post and he threw the wrapper away."

"Did she know he was prone to epileptic fits?"

"Yes, but he made her promise not to tell anyone."

After Agatha had rung off, she told Toni what Patrick had said.

"Someone knew about his fits," said Toni, "and someone evil decided to mess with his brain."

"Let's get back to concentrating on the blackmail idea," said Agatha. "Now, the vicar's wife would be terrified of scandal. But what about our lady of the manor, Sam Framington? She was an actress. Maybe someone found out something about her past."

"Shall we go and see her?"

"I think it would be a waste of time," said Agatha. "I've got contacts in the media in London. I'll go up there for a few days and see what I can dig up."

"Will I stay on here?" asked Toni.

"No, better not. Just not safe."

Agatha went back home that evening. Before she let herself into her cottage, she looked across at James's home. But it was all in darkness and his car was not parked outside.

She patted her cats and then switched on her computer and typed in the name Samantha Wilkes. Sam, when she had worked as an actress, had enjoyed only one steady run of work, a part in a television soap called *Yesterday's Family* where she played the role of a village femme fatale. The soap had been produced by Zetlik Television. Agatha looked them up, took a note of their address and decided to visit them on the following day.

She had a sudden longing to see Mrs. Bloxby and listen to her calm voice. The vicar's wife was about the only person Agatha trusted. She had once seen a card in a shop over the till stating "In God we trust. Others pay cash," and Agatha thought that summed up her philosophy. It never dawned on her that she expected too much of herself and therefore expected high standards from everyone else and so was bound to be disappointed.

She did not phone the vicarage first because she knew the vicar might answer and tell her his wife was not at home because Agatha knew he did not like her.

To her relief, Mrs. Bloxby herself answered the door and invited her in. The evening had turned chilly. A log fire crackled in the grate. A standard lamp cast a golden glow over the shabby but comfortable room. Agatha sank gratefully down into the feather-stuffed cushions of the sofa, accepted a gin and tonic, and began to tell Mrs. Bloxby about all the latest developments.

"Poor Mr. Summer," exclaimed Mrs. Bloxby. "I am sure he did not start taking those wretched mushrooms by chance. I am sure someone persuaded him that they would help his epilepsy. What a dangerous, callous and evil person."

"I think that someone might be blackmailing people in the village," said Agatha.

"Out of the people you have interviewed, who might it be?"

"It would need to be someone people had confided in at one time," said Agatha. "The only person I can think of is the vicar. There is confession in the Church of England, isn't there? I didn't see a confession box in the church."

"It is not like the Roman Catholic Church, but, yes, if someone feels burdened with a sin they can talk to a member of the clergy. But what about the landlord of the pub? That seems to be the village meeting place. He might know a lot about everyone. People gossip in pubs. And in village shops."

Agatha suddenly remembered the bitter old woman in the village shop.

"You've given me a lot to think about," she said. "I suppose James is still on his travels."

"I believe so. Poor Miss Gilmour. Such a shame."

"She really must get over this penchant for older men," said Agatha huffily.

"Miss Gilmour has had a difficult time in her young life," said Mrs. Bloxby. "I suppose all women at one time or another look for a sort of father figure."

"I don't fancy much older men," said Agatha.

Mrs. Bloxby repressed a smile. At Agatha's age, much older men would really have passed the bounds of being sexually attractive.

"I must go," said Agatha. "Thanks for listening."

Agatha presented herself at the Soho offices of Zetlik Television the next day and asked where she could find the producer of *Yesterday's Family*. The receptionist told her to wait. Agatha sat down and skimmed through a magazine, reflecting it was surely a sign of age when you did not know who half the celebrities were.

At last, the receptionist returned with a small, portly man who introduced himself as the personnel manager. "You want Jack Kyncaid," he said. "But he retired five years ago. What do you want him for?"

Agatha passed over her card. "I wanted to ask him about the time he worked with Samantha Wilkes. I need the background of everyone connected with a murder case I am investigating."

"I suppose there's no harm in letting you talk to him. Poor old soul is always hanging around hoping for work. Sad."

"Where can I find him?"

He looked at his watch. "He'll be in the pub on the corner on your left as you go out."

"How will I recognise him?"

He laughed. "Can't miss him. He had a thick head of grey hair and he's just dyed it blond."

Agatha thanked him and made her way to the pub. Jack Kyncaid was sitting at a table under a wall light which shone off his bright yellow head of hair. But Agatha noted that he was perhaps only a little older than she was herself. He was a small man, dressed casually in a suede jacket and jeans over a faded black T-shirt. He had small black eyes in a pale face, a long thin mouth and a large nose.

Again, Agatha handed over a card and explained what she wanted to know. "Sit down," he said. "It's quite a time ago."

"May I get you a drink?" said Agatha.

"A double Scotch, please."

Agatha went to the bar and ordered it and a gin and tonic for herself and then returned to join him.

"Now," said Agatha, "what do you remember about Samantha Wilkes, now Lady Framington?"

"She was playing the part of a parlour maid who

gets seduced by his lordship," said Jack. "That was a right joke. She was pretty much seduced by most of the male cast. Mind you, she was a looker. I saw a photo of her when she got married and I could hardly recognise her. Gone all county. But she got her title at last."

"At last?" prompted Agatha.

"Mind if I have another one of these?"

Agatha hurried to the bar and elbowed her way through the lunchtime crowd. She returned with his drink and fastened her bearlike eyes on him.

"You were saying something about she got her title at last."

"When we were on location at this mansion, she set her cap at his lordship, who was pretty ancient. Her ladyship stepped in and threatened to turn us all out if we didn't get rid of her so she was written out."

"Where was this?"

"Big sprawling place in the Cotswolds, near Broadway."

"What was the name of the family?"

"Crighton? No, that's not it. Ah, I remember. Craton."

With a jolt, Agatha remembered that Mrs. Tripp had been cook at Lady Craton's.

"I must say I was sorry for Sam," said Jack. "She wept buckets. But she went on to get a few parts here and there. It's a wicked business, the media. Here am

I with all my years of experience, out on the scrap heap."

"Maybe you could retrain in some other field," suggested Agatha.

He gave her a sour look. "See. It's like the joke of a couple watching a man shovelling elephant shit at a circus. They ask him, 'Why don't you get a decent job?' And he says, 'What! And leave show business?'"

Agatha drove back to Carsely, stopping only at Beaconsfield for a sandwich and a cup of coffee.

She found Charles ensconced in her living room, watching television, with her cats on his lap.

"Listen to this!" cried Agatha, dumping herself down on the sofa next to him and easing her feet out of her high heels. She told him all Jack Kyncaid had said.

"So she's probably a blackmailer," said Charles. "But a murderer? And why Gloria French?"

"I don't know," said Agatha. "I mean she's old. She can't exactly nip about the place unseen."

"Is there a road at the back of Gloria's cottage?"

"I remember, there's a lane."

"She's got a mobility scooter."

"What! I never saw her on it."

"I noticed it one day we were down there. It was

parked at the side of her cottage. She could nip around the place on that."

"I wonder what Lady Craton died of," said Agatha. She went to her computer and switched it on. After a few minutes, she said, "Got it. A heart attack. Just like Jerry. Oh God, maybe she bumped her off in order to benefit in the will."

"What's the name of the Craton place?"

"Five Trees Manor. Been there?"

"No. I wonder if it still exists. Let's go down there tomorrow morning and have a look."

Five Trees Manor turned out to be now the headquarters of the Golden Age Insurance Company. It lay on the road between Snows Hill and Broadway. A good part of what had once been the estate was now a housing complex.

Farther down the road towards Broadway were two cottages. Agatha knocked at the door of the first one and asked the woman who answered if she knew of anyone still alive who had once worked for the Craton family.

The woman's round, rosy country face creased in thought. "Wait there," she said finally. "I'll ask Mother."

Only an occasional car passed on the road behind them. A beautiful yellow rosebush stood beside the door.

At last she came back. "Mother's bedridden and can't come down the stairs. She says old Mrs. Grey next door used to work at the manor ages ago."

They rang the bell at the door of the next cottage. A small, bent, elderly woman opened it up and peered up at them. Agatha explained they wanted to talk to someone who had once worked at the manor.

"I did," she said. "Come in. I'm Rose Grey." She led the way into a small, hot parlour, cluttered with odds and ends of furniture. She eased herself painfully into an armchair and motioned to them to sit down.

"It must be twenty-five years ago when the old lady died," she said. "I was working as a cleaner, going in daily with some other women to do the rough work."

"Do you remember the cook, Mrs. Tripp?"

"Yes, she was about to be pensioned off when Lady Craton died. His lordship died the year before and they had no children. A cousin inherited and sold the lot. Gladys Tripp was making a song and dance about losing her job, saying she was still fit. But the fact was that Lady Craton said she could get caterers in when she had people to stay and couldn't afford to keep on any full-time staff."

"Do you remember when a television company used the manor as a location?"

"Of course. Right excited everyone was."

"Do you remember an actress called Samantha Wilkes?"

"Oh, yes," said Rose with a smile. "She chased anything in trousers and then set her cap at old Lord Craton. He got quite dotty about her and my lady was flaming mad and got rid of her. Then there was a big scandal when it turned out my lord had given this actress his wife's pearls as a present. Lady Craton tried but couldn't get them back."

"Did Mrs. Tripp inherit anything in Lady Craton's will?"

"She got twenty thousand pounds and a few pieces of antique furniture. The cousin said the furniture wasn't mentioned in the will, but Gladys had a letter signed by Lady Craton, promising her the pieces."

"Did you like her?"

"Not a bit. At first she was all cosy and friendly. Liked to get people to talk about themselves. Then she went right off me. Always seemed to be standing over me, supervising my work. Now, that actress flirted disgracefully with his old lordship and he was so taken with her. And Gladys Tripp seemed to be encouraging her, passing notes from Samantha to his lordship. Then one day in the kitchen, Gladys and Samantha had this terrible row. Seems her ladyship got hold of one of those letters and was screaming blue murder. Next thing is Samantha is sent packing.

"Her ladyship was in such a state, we were frightened she'd have a heart attack. The vicar was sent for . . ."

"Vicar?" demanded Agatha. "What was his name?"

"Let me think. Tall, thin chap. Married a girl from Broadway. Some scandal there but I can't bring it to mind."

"What church was that?"

"St. Paul's."

"Did Lady Craton have a weak heart?" asked Charles.

"I would have said she was as strong as an ox. But some time after his lordship died, she suddenly had this heart attack."

Agatha leaned forward. "Did Mrs. Tripp make home remedies in the kitchen, you know, country cures for illnesses?"

"That she did. Always out in the fields and woods looking for plants. I didn't like her. I thought she was a bit creepy. Oily, like."

They left after having decided that Rose Grey had told them as much as she knew. Agatha phoned Mrs. Bloxby and asked her to check if Guy Enderbury had ever been a vicar at St. Paul's.

"Let's go for lunch," said Agatha. "I can't believe all this. Old Mrs. Tripp. It's not possible. She seems to sleep most of the time."

They were just starting their lunch when Mrs. Bloxby phoned with the news that Guy Enderbury had indeed once been the vicar of St. Paul's.

"Look at it this way," said Agatha after she had told Charles the latest news. "She's just not spry enough to nip round to Gloria's, get down to the cellar and nip back again."

"I think it's time you told the police," said Charles. "They'll do a search of her home. Say she kept those notes from Sam to Lord Craton and was blackmailing her."

"I found out all this," said Agatha stubbornly. "And the police aren't going to take the glory away from me."

"It's no good going back to watch her," said Charles. "If it's all an act, she'll play it to the hilt. None of us can go. We've all been down there, apart from Patrick, and no matter what that man does to himself, he'll always look like a policeman."

Agatha stabbed her fork viciously into a steak and ale pie. A little fountain of gravy shot up into her face.

"Snakes and bastards!" shouted Agatha.

"Oh, wipe your face and shut up," said Charles. "I can't think."

Agatha went off to the loo to repair her make-up. When she returned, Charles said, "I've just phoned James. He's back. I said we would go and see him."

"James?"

"Why not? He's done some detective work for you before. He might jump at the chance of working for you to redeem his character in your eyes. Can you think of anything else?"

"As long as he keeps in touch," said Agatha.

"You mean, you don't want him solving the case before you get to take the credit?"

"No," lied Agatha. "I just don't want him getting poisoned."

Chapter Seven

James looked at them nervously when he opened the door. Charles had said they just needed to talk to him and he was bracing himself for a lecture. He had broken off his researches abroad to return and give Mary a full apology.

Inside every man is a small boy. In James Lacey's case it was hardly ever evident. But Agatha saw the pleading look in his eyes like a child waiting to be punished and said quickly, "I need your help on a case, James."

His face cleared and he said heartily, "Come in! Come in! I'll do anything I can to help."

Agatha looked around the familiar book-lined living room. It was hard to believe she had ever been married to James. He had done practically nothing, she remembered, to change his bachelor ways.

He served them with coffee and then Agatha outlined what she had found out about the whole murder case, and how, as everyone she could think of had been to the village already, she was hoping James would go and see what he could find out.

James hesitated. "I really only came back for a couple of days to do something."

"I hope you're not too upset about Mary Gotobed getting married," said Agatha.

Relief flooded James's handsome face. "Really? That's great. I mean . . . *really*? Who to?"

"Some farmer over in Ebrington."

"Well, come to think of it, I suppose I could go down to Piddlebury and have a look around," said James.

"What I really want to know," said Agatha, "is how she could possibly get around. She walks with the aid of sticks."

"What about a mobility scooter," said James. "You know, one of those electric chair things. Some of them can go up to thirty miles per hour."

"I didn't see one," said Agatha. "Mind you, I wasn't looking for it. But Charles saw one parked at the side of her house."

"Let me have a copy of your notes," said James. "I'll go over them tonight and get down there tomorrow. Who am I supposed to be?"

"A hearty rambler would be a good idea," said Charles.

"What if I just go as myself and say I'm writing a travel book on the pubs of England?"

"Bad idea," said Charles. "Book into the Green Man under another name. Mrs. Tripp may not be able to use a computer but someone curious about you in that village would only need to Google James Lacey to find out who you are and that at one time you were married to Aggie here."

"Oh, all right. But I hate fake names."

"What about keeping James and make your second name Laney?" suggested Agatha.

"Too close," protested Charles. "What about James Stanton? You can think of the Cotswold village of Stanton Lacey and that'll remind you of your alias."

James did not relish the idea of hiking all the way to Piddlebury. Instead, he left his car at Mircester and set out from there. He suddenly saw Toni at the other side of the car park. She saw him, too. They both stood for a moment and then James waved and strode off. It's not only age but sheer embarrassment that separates us now, he thought.

The day was unusually warm for mid-October. Newspapers reported records were being broken. People wrote to the *Times* about their roses having a second flowering. He was suitably tired and dusty looking by the time he arrived at the Green Man. Moses welcomed him and showed him to his room.

"You'll have heard about the murders here," he said.

"I've just come back from abroad and I hadn't been reading the newspapers," said James. "What murders?"

"Some maniac from outside the village killed a couple of people," said Moses. "But it's all nice and quiet now."

"Get someone for it?" asked James, dumping his rucksack on the floor.

"No, but it's all over and done with."

James wanted to point out that unsolved murders in a small village like this could hardly be said to be over and done with, but did not want to betray too much curiosity.

And knowing the psychology of villagers, he was sure if he did not ask questions and continued to seem uninterested, then people might talk to him.

James had no vanity about his looks but the fact that a very handsome man was staying at the inn spread rapidly round the village. Despite the heat of the day, the evening was chilly and the bar was set out as a dining room. James cast a jaundiced eye over the usual pub grub offered on the blackboard menu behind the bar and ordered lasagne without chips, collected a glass of lager and sat down at a corner table near the window.

The room began to fill up. James ate his lasagne, ordered coffee and then barricaded himself behind a book. The waves of curiosity surrounding him felt almost tangible. At last, the bar, which had been pretty silent, became filled with conversation. Two farmers were complaining bitterly about the poor fruit harvest. A pretty girl with an older man were talking about a series on television. James guessed the pretty girl and her friend were Peter Suncliff and Jenny Soper. He heard several voices greet a newcomer. "Evening, Lady Framington," and "Evening, Sam. You don't eat here usually."

"Felt I had to get out. Oh, there doesn't seem to be a free table. No, don't get up. I'm sure that nice man over there won't mind if I join him."

James looked up as Sam approached his table. "Do you mind if I join you?" she asked.

"Please do. Actually, I was just about to leave."

"Oh, you can't do that," said Sam. "Stay for a little. We don't get many visitors." She held out her hand. "I'm Sam."

"And I'm James," said James, grateful for the use of first names because it had temporarily slipped his mind what his surname was supposed to be.

Amazing how some people's looks change when

they get older, thought James. No one would believe that Sam had once been an attractive actress. The cropped iron grey hair and tailored linen suit fitted the lady of the manor. The trout pout, painted pillar box red, hinted at the onetime vamp.

Moses came out from behind the bar. "Get you anything, Lady Framington?"

"I think I'll just have a glass of wine. What are you having, James?"

"I've got coffee to finish, but thanks all the same."

"So what brings you to our little village?" said Sam.

"Just doing a walking tour. A holiday."

"And what do you do when you're not on holiday?"

Silence had fallen in the pub as if everyone was waiting to hear James's reply.

"I'm a computer programmer. I'm between contracts, actually."

"Aren't you nervous you won't get any more work with everything being outsourced to India?"

James smiled. "No, I always get something."

Moses put Sam's drink down beside her. "Cheers," she said. "Look, why don't you come back to my place for a nightcap? My house is . . ."

Her voice trailed away. The bar had fallen silent except for the thump, thump, thump of two sticks.

James had his back to the room. He swung round.

An elderly lady had stopped in the middle of the bar. He thought that she looked like the bad fairy turning up at the christening in *Sleeping Beauty*. She was wearing a long black dress and her black eyes peered maliciously round the room before settling on James.

As she shuffled forward, Sam let out a sort of squawk of alarm, rose abruptly, said, "I left something in the oven," and fled out of the pub.

Mrs. Tripp eased herself down into Sam's vacated chair, and said, "Welcome to Piddlebury. What's your name?"

"James Stanton."

"And what's your business here?"

"Minding my own. Sorry to desert you, but I've had a long walk."

"Rambling, are you?"

"I'm perfectly coherent," said James, wondering why he was antagonising her. He reminded himself severely that he was supposed to be a detective. "I can wait a bit," he said. "May I get you a drink?"

"Moses knows what I like." The owner was already approaching with a glass of dark liquid.

"How much do I owe you?" asked James.

"On the house," said Moses.

"This is pretty good port," said Mrs. Tripp. "You look like an army man."

"Not me," said James. "I am just a walker trying to have a relaxing walk through Gloucestershire. Have you lived here all your life?"

"Was brought up here. Went into service for Lady Craton over at Broadway. Worked for her right into my seventies, I did. I was her cook."

"You had two murders in this village, I've heard."

Her black eyes suddenly seemed to bore into him. "Hard to miss. Was all over the papers and the telly, too."

"I was abroad," said James. "I didn't read the newspapers. I only heard about the murders when I got here."

She finished her drink with one gulp. Then she rose to her feet and farted loudly. "Help me to my cottage," she ordered.

She handed James one of her sticks and then grabbed his arm. She smelled awful. This is like *Night of the Living Dead*, thought James, fighting down a feeling of revulsion.

Sam was on the phone to Clarice. "He's a most divine man," she was saying, "but Ma Tripp came tottering in so I fled. You must meet him. He might be at the service tomorrow. If he is, grab him and bring him to the manor for a drink afterwards."

James phoned Agatha before he went to bed. "I saw a mobility scooter beside her cottage so she could certainly zip around in that. She wanted me to go into her cottage with her, but the smell of her was making me feel sick."

"I don't remember her smelling all that bad," said Agatha.

"She farted in the pub and the smell seemed to hang about."

"I wonder if she took an overdose of laxative herself," said Agatha. "Some people think they're cleaning out their systems with the stuff. You'd better get along to the church tomorrow and have a look at everyone."

When James attended the morning service, he was relieved to see Mrs. Tripp was not among the congregation and then felt like a bad detective. He thought a lot of the women were dressed up as if for a wedding, not knowing that they had put on their best finery having heard about the handsome newcomer.

Agatha had described the vicar's wife as having red hair. James noticed her sitting in one of the front pews next to Sam.

Sun slanted through the stained-glass windows,

sending harlequins of light dancing over the interior of the church. James's mind started to wander during the service. The vicar, clutching the spread wings of the brass eagle which held the Bible, was ranting on about something from Revelation. Then he said something which caught James's attention. From the notes, he remembered the vicar was waiting for God to tell him the identity of the murderer. "God has at last spoken to me," said Guy Enderbury. "This village will soon be cleansed of evil."

There was a sort of communal gasp, then a shuffling of feet as the congregation rose to sing the final hymn.

James remained seated at the end of the service. He wanted to have a quiet word with the vicar when everyone had gone. Sam stopped and smiled down at him. "Do come to the manor for a drink."

"I'll follow you," said James. "I like churches. I would like to sit here for a bit."

"I hope he's not religious," said Clarice as she walked in the direction of the manor with Sam. "I get enough of that from my husband."

"Do you think he really knows the identity of the murderer?" said Sam.

"Not for a moment. If you ask me, he's going weird," said Clarice.

James was the last to leave the church. He shook hands with Guy and said, "That was a very startling statement you made."

"I am surprised you should find a sermon on Revelation startling."

"I meant about knowing the identity of the murderer. And shouldn't you tell the police?"

"What would they say?" Guy shrugged. "When I tell them that God revealed the identity of the murderer to me, all they would do is suggest psychiatric help."

James was puzzled. The vicar did seem perfectly sane. "But aren't you worried that the murderer might now target you?"

"That is what I am hoping," said the vicar calmly.

"I think, you know, that God did not talk to you at all," said James. "I think you are hoping that the murderer will come after you and then you will really know who it is."

"Another unbeliever," said Guy with a laugh. "You must come to the vicarage one evening."

"You are very kind. I do not know how long I'll be staying."

James walked off in the direction of the manor house. Thanks to Agatha's copious notes, he knew exactly where it was.

That afternoon, Agatha was sitting in Carsely's vicarage garden, drinking tea. She had been summoned by Mrs. Bloxby. "So what did you really want to see me about?" she asked after Mrs. Bloxby had finished describing various events in the parish.

"I really try to avoid gossip," said Mrs. Bloxby, "but on your behalf, I made some enquiries about the time Mr. Enderbury was vicar in Broadway. There is something there in his history."

"Let's have it." Agatha looked at a scone brimming with fresh cream and strawberry jam. She gave a little sigh and decided to leave it alone.

"Clarice Phelps, as she was then, was waitress in a pub which did bar lunches. By all accounts, she chased after the vicar. She lived in a room above the pub which was accessed by a back stair. On several evenings, the vicar was spotted going up those stairs and tongues began to wag. Then the couple were seen one day having a scene outside the church. Clarice was crying. Two days later she was taken off to hospital. A nurse gossiped. Clarice had taken some potion which had caused an abortion. Whatever it was caused such damage that she was told she would not be able to bear children. Mr. Enderbury married her when she got out of hospital and shortly afterwards moved out of Broadway."

Agatha's eyes gleamed. "That's the connection. She probably went to Mrs. Tripp for something to help her abort. But would she succumb to blackmail? I mean, if it had all been gossiped about before?"

"But no one in Piddlebury would know about it—except Mrs. Tripp—and believe me, a vicar's wife is supposed to be above reproach. Are you sure James is safe?"

"I hope so. Why do you ask?"

"What if someone in Piddlebury wonders if there is any connection to you and looks up your history on the Internet? They will find reports of your marriage to James and a photograph of him."

Agatha groaned. "I never thought of that. I'd better phone him and get him out of there."

James was in his room in the pub when Agatha rang him. He listened to her news and then Mrs. Bloxby's suggestion that anyone with a computer could find out his real identity.

"I'll be safe as long as I don't drink or eat anything out of the way," said James. "The vicar made an announcement in the church that God had told him the identity of the murderer."

"That man's as daft as a brush."

"I don't think so," said James. "I think he's hoping

to lure the murderer. I'm going to be watching him. Clarice and Sam have been flirting with me like mad. I had drinks at the manor after the service."

"Oh, I do wish you'd leave."

"I'll give it a couple of days."

After Agatha had rung off, her phone rang again. It was Roy Silver. "Any news?" he asked.

"About the murders? Strange as it seems, the prime suspect is old Mrs. Tripp."

"Can't be," jeered Roy. "She couldn't keep awake long enough."

"What if that falling asleep is all an act?" asked Agatha.

"She's ancient. I wouldn't mind getting my hands on some of her furniture."

"I hardly noticed. Everything is covered in framed photos."

"Well, there's a desk which looks like Sheraton. My friend, Tristram, told me lots about antique furniture. There's a console table in her little hall to die for. There's a fortune hidden under all those photos and bits and pieces."

Agatha suddenly remembered the chest of drawers in Gloria's cottage. Had Gloria borrowed it and not given it back? And what excuse would she give for having borrowed it? The whole village would have seen it being transported.

"Got to go," said Agatha hurriedly.

She phoned James back and told him about the furniture and the chest of drawers she had seen in Gloria's home. "Gloria used Henry Bruce for odd jobs," said Agatha. "Get along there and ask him if he ever moved a chest of drawers from Mrs. Tripp's house to Gloria's."

James checked his notes again and set off for Henry's cottage. The leaves on the trees in the wood above the village were turning red and gold. The Indian summer was drawing to an end. There was a chill in the air and the sun above was a pale disk.

Henry was tinkering with the engine of an old Ford when James arrived outside his cottage.

"Mr. Bruce?" Henry straightened up, wiping his hands on an oily rag. In that moment, James realised that direct questioning would blow his cover.

"I'm looking for an old banger," he said. "Someone in the shop said you might have something."

Henry grinned. "I should have this here finished by the end of the day."

"How many miles on the clock?"

"One hundred and twenty-seven."

"It'll go all right?"

"Tired of walking?"

"It's a long road home," said James.

"And where's home?"

James stopped himself just in time from saying "Carsely."

"Evesham," he said.

"Whereabouts in Evesham?"

"What a lot of questions," said James. "If you must know, it's one of those villas round from the Regal Cinema."

"Come inside," said Henry. "We'll have a beer."

James followed him into the kitchen, wondering all the while how to bring the subject round to Mrs. Tripp.

They sat at the kitchen table. "How much for the car?" asked James as Henry brought two bottles of beer from the fridge.

"Five hundred—cash."

"How old is it?"

"Nine years."

"Give me a couple of days to think about it."

Henry shrugged. "Suit yourself. Do you do a lot of these walking tours?"

"This is like being interrogated by the police," said James testily. "Why all these damn questions?"

"It's like this," said Henry. "There's been two murders in this village and we're sure it was done by some stranger. Stands to reason we're nervous about strangers."

"Why a stranger?" asked James. "Aren't there any weird people in this village? There was an old woman came into the pub last night and the way people reacted you'd think she'd arrived straight out of hell."

"That'd be Mrs. Tripp. She's harmless."

"Really? Do any work for her?"

"I keep clear, see. She likes people to read to her. I mind when she wanted me to move something to Gloria's . . ."

"Wasn't one of the murdered people called Gloria?"

"Right. Anyway, I'd just got it on the trolley, when she says, 'Read to me.' I told her right out I was being paid to move the drawers, not read."

"Why on earth would Gloria want to borrow a chest of drawers of all things?"

"Seems that our lady of the manor twigged Gloria for having a house full of cheap drek and Gloria wanted to show her she had something good."

"That's crazy," said James. "I mean, don't you find that odd?"

"Well, our Gloria was so pushy that people just did what she wanted to shut her up."

"Anyway, did Mrs. Tripp get her chest of drawers back?"

"Don't know."

Sam and Clarice were deep in conversation. "I don't think he looks like a rambler," said Clarice. "He seemed keen to find out about our murders."

"Well, anyone would," said Sam. "But I'll look up the Internet and see if there's anything on him." She went to her desk and powered up her computer. "Let me see . . . James Stanton. Several here." She clicked away. "Not our man."

"Look up Agatha Raisin," said Clarice.

"Why?"

"Just a hunch."

"Okay." Sam's fingers clicked busily across the keys. "She's had quite a life. Married James Lacey."

"Oh! Try James Lacey."

The keys rattled. "Here we are. It's our man! He's a writer of military histories and travel books. He must be here snooping for the Raisin woman."

James phoned Agatha with the latest news. When he had finished, Agatha said, "Don't go near Mrs. Tripp."

"You mean she might have bumped off Gloria because she couldn't get her chest of drawers back?"

"She's so sinister, she might have done it. James. I think you should leave now! It's not safe."

"But look at all I've found out. I'm sure I can crack this case for you."

"James, please."

"Another couple of days."

James Lacey was usually a very pragmatic, level-headed man apart from a few occasions in his life, one of which had been his temporary infatuation with Toni. He still felt ashamed of his behaviour. It was this very shame that drove him on to want to solve the murders. He felt that would somehow be a way to redeem himself.

He decided to go out for a stroll before dinner. The main street of the little village was deserted. How odd, he thought, that such a beautiful little secluded place should harbour a murderer.

The first stars were appearing in a pale green sky. The air was redolent of a mixture of cooking smells and flowers. The evening air was pure and clean. He stopped in the street and took a deep breath.

That was when something struck him viciously in the back of the legs and sent him flying on his face onto the cobbles. He scrambled to his feet and turned round.

Mrs. Tripp was crouched over the controls of her mobility scooter. "I'm sorry," she said. "Didn't see you standing there."

"You should be glad I don't seem to have broken anything," raged James, "or I would have sued you."

"My eyes aren't what they used to be," said the old

lady. "Follow me to my cottage. I can give you the very thing to soothe any hurts."

Why not? thought James. Here we go, into the lioness's den.

"I'll follow you," he said.

"I'll get it ready," said Mrs. Tripp. "I'll leave the door open."

She turned her scooter and sped off.

James followed. He spotted, out of the corner of his eye, several cottage curtains twitching as he walked past. In the sky above, thin fingers of dark cloud were beginning to trail across it and a chill little wind had sprung up.

Does she plan to poison me? he wondered. Surely not. What on earth would she do with the body? I'm a big man. Besides, my stuff is at the inn. Better just pretend to drink anything she offers me.

Her cottage door stood open but the cottage itself seemed to be in blackness.

"Are you in there?" he called.

"The lights have gone," came the old lady's voice. "The fuse box is in the kitchen over the sink. The kitchen's at the back."

James groped his way along a narrow, stone-flagged passage. The kitchen was faintly lit by the pale light of the dying day outside. A rising wind began to moan eerily around the old cottage. He stood on a rug on the middle of the floor and reached for the fuse box. The rug gave way and he plunged down into a hole. His hand caught an old iron handle at the side and he hung on and then felt the handle slowly begin to give way. He shouted for help. It must be an old well, he thought. He braced his legs on either side and tried to make his way up. It was then he heard the sound of two sets of footsteps. He looked up. The faint round of the hole above disappeared as something heavy was dragged across it with a scraping sound.

James decided to see if he could make his way down and hope the well was dry. Then all he could do was to sit at the bottom and hope that his absence would prompt Agatha to alert the police. He slithered down, trying to break a headlong fall by grabbing hold of worn bits of masonry. At last he touched bottom. At least it was dry. His phone! He had forgotten his phone. He took it out of his pocket and dialled nine-nine-nine but there was no signal.

He began to shout for help until he was hoarse.

Chapter Eight

Agatha had received a text message from James the previous night, which she read before going to bed. She was always glad when texts were written in clear English because she had difficulty managing to read text-type English. It said, "Going out for a walk to look around. Going to keep an eye on Mrs. Tripp."

In the morning, again worried about James, Agatha tried to phone him without success. She phoned the Green Man. Moses said he hadn't been down for breakfast. Agatha didn't want to leave her name and blow his cover. Still worried, she went to the vicarage and asked Mrs. Bloxby to call.

Mrs. Bloxby got the same reply. Persevering, she asked Moses to go up to his room and tell him to call Mrs. Bloxby. Both women waited in anxious silence.

At last, Moses came back on the phone. "He's gone," he said crossly. "Took his rucksack with him and left without paying."

When Mrs. Bloxby told Agatha what Moses had said, Agatha said, "They've murdered him. I should have told the police."

"Tell them now," urged Mrs. Bloxby.

Agatha phoned Bill Wong and outlined all she had found out about Mrs. Tripp and begged him to get down there with a search warrant.

"You haven't given me enough to get permission for a search warrant," said Bill. "But don't worry. Anyone going missing in that village demands investigation. We'll be down there right away."

Agatha told Mrs. Bloxby that the police were going to Piddlebury but said, "I'll get there first. They must have found out who he was. I'll get there before Bill cuts through the red tape."

Breaking the speed limit, Agatha raced to Piddle-bury and screeched to a halt outside Mrs. Tripp's cottage. She hammered on the door and rang the bell. She was just picking up a rock to break a glass panel on the door and force her way in when it opened.

Mrs. Tripp stood leering up at her. "Back again?"

"Where is he?"

"Who?"

"Mr. Stanton."

"You'd best ask at the inn."

The door began to close. Agatha stuck her foot in it. "I want to come in and look."

"Well, you can't."

"Let me in!"

Mrs. Tripp stood aside. "Very well. You can read to me."

Agatha shoved past her. The noise from the television set was blaring throughout the house. She looked around the parlour. Mrs. Tripp is not deaf, she thought suddenly. She switched off the television. That was when she thought she heard a faint cry. Mrs. Tripp was standing in the doorway of the parlour.

"That's enough," said the old lady. "Get out."

"What's up, old girl? I got your phone call." Henry Bruce had appeared behind her.

"It's that detective, that's what. We need to get rid of her."

"I've done enough."

"You forget. If I go down, I'll damn well take you with me."

Henry moved into the parlour and advanced on Agatha.

Agatha looked wildly around for a weapon. She seized handfuls of photographs in silver frames and began to hurl them at him, screaming all the while for help at the top of her voice. Blood began to pour from a cut in Henry's forehead where the edge of a silver frame had caught him. Temporarily blinded, he staggered back. Agatha darted round him for the doorway. That was when Mrs. Tripp swung one of her sticks and brought it down on Agatha's head.

Agatha fell to the floor. "Now, help me," panted Mrs. Tripp. "Shove her down the well."

Henry mopped the blood from his forehead with an oily handkerchief. He seized Agatha by the ankles and began to drag her towards the kitchen.

James heard the scraping sound of someone trying to remove the well cover. If only he could get up there and dive out of the hole. He was grateful for his mountaineering days that had taught him to climb a chimney. Bracing his arms and legs on either side of the well, he began to move slowly upwards.

"This is heavy," he heard a man's voice complain. "Do you really want me to throw her down on top of him?"

"Nasty, snooping bitch," came Mrs. Tripp's voice. "They can die together."

Then there came a howl of pain. "She's come round. She kicked me in the balls."

The sound of a whack. "That's put her out," said Mrs. Tripp. "Stop leaping about and chuck the damn woman down the well."

I hope it's not Agatha, thought James as he heaved himself ever upwards.

The scraping started again. With one final heave, James got himself to nearly the top. When the cover was pulled back, fuelled by a sort of mad desperation, James tumbled out onto the kitchen floor. Mrs. Tripp screamed. Henry tried to kick James back down the hole. James rushed forward and butted Henry in the stomach and sent him flying against a Welsh dresser.

Weak from his ordeal down the well, James collapsed on the floor.

Sick and faint, Agatha opened her eyes to see Mrs. Tripp swinging her stick to bring it down on James's head. With one monumental heave, she got to her knees and seized the old woman by the ankles, making her lose balance, and then she lost consciousness again.

At that moment, police headed by Bill Wong rushed into the house. They heard a cry from James.

Bill could hardly believe the scene in the kitchen that met his eyes. Mrs. Tripp was lying on the floor, moaning that Agatha had broken her hip, Henry Bruce had got to his feet and was as white as a sheet, James was sitting on the floor with his head in his hands and Agatha had blood pouring from a wound in her head. James looked up when he saw Bill and said, "Arrest Henry Bruce and Mrs. Tripp. They tried to kill both of us."

Agatha recovered consciousness later that day in hospital in Mircester. She looked groggily at Bill and Alice Peterson.

"Feeling well enough to talk?" asked Bill.

"Don't know. Feel woozy and sick," said Agatha. "Have you got them?"

"Yes, Bruce is singing like a canary. He claims that Ma Tripp was incandescent because Gloria wouldn't hand back her bureau. She got Bruce to nip down to the cellar and put the poisoned bottle in the crate. Clever old biddy told him to wear larger shoes. She knew Gloria was upset by the scene in the village shop and knew she would head for the bottle."

"Wait a minute," said Agatha faintly. "Right up to the last minute Gloria was expecting the vicar and his wife. Didn't she care whether she poisoned them as well?"

"Clarice was in the shop just after Gloria had left.

She told everyone she'd remembered that she and Guy were to have drinks with Gloria and said she was rushing back to get her husband to cancel it. Evidently Mrs. Tripp calculated that Gloria really would head for the bottle. Bruce was told to wait and listen for any sounds of distress from Gloria. When he heard them, he was to get the bottle and glass and get rid of both."

"We think that's why we didn't catch them before," said Alice. "So hit-and-miss. So amateur and yet so cunning. Bruce disabled Roy's car and put the digitalis that Mrs. Tripp had brewed up in his flask. Another hit-and-miss plan."

Agatha raised a hand to her bandaged head in bewilderment. "But the whole village must have been covering for them."

"We're still going through her papers. Both Sam and Clarice had a fling with Henry Bruce. They were being blackmailed. It was nothing to do with their time in Broadway."

"How did you find that out?" asked Agatha. "I mean, no one writes letters these days. Did Sam and Clarice tell you about it?"

"We haven't questioned them yet," said Bill. "It was all on dear Henry's computer. Moses Green was threatened by having lock-ins, you know the villagers drinking long after hours. That explains why he was so anxious to get rid of you."

"What about poor Jerry Tarrant?" asked Agatha.

"He was gay."

"So what?" demanded Agatha.

"It obviously mattered a lot to him. Henry Bruce had been clubbing in Birmingham and saw him going into a gay club."

"Are you now exhuming his body?"

"He was cremated."

"Snakes and bastards," said Agatha sleepily. "I wish Mrs. Tripp weren't so old. I'd like her to rot in prison for years." Her eyes began to close.

"We'll leave you to rest," said Bill.

Agatha's eyes jerked open. "But what about the rest of the village, all insisting it was someone from outside?"

"We're working on that. Go to sleep. You'll be all right. The hospital says you've a head like iron."

The following day, Agatha felt much better and was delighted to receive a visit from Mrs. Bloxby after she had made an official statement to Bill.

"It's quite a sensation," said the vicar's wife. "It's all over the newspapers and television."

The door of Agatha's room opened and Toni and Simon came in. "We've called before," said Toni, "but you were asleep and we were told not to disturb you."

Agatha told them what Bill had said. "What evil!" exclaimed Mrs. Bloxby.

"I know," said Agatha. "It almost makes city crime look clean by comparison."

"Patrick, Phil and Mrs. Freedman have all been round," said Toni. "You were asleep then so they were told not to disturb you."

"Everyone seems to have brought a lot of goodies," said Agatha, eyeing the baskets of fruit and boxes of chocolate. "Have you seen James or Charles?"

"Not yet," said Mrs. Bloxby, studying the bleak view outside the hospital window.

"You look awkward," said Agatha sharply. "Out with it!"

"I phoned and told Mr. Lacey I was going to visit you and asked if he would like to come. He said, 'Not now. Maybe later.'"

Two days later, Agatha received the glad news that she was to be allowed home. Her hospital room was crammed with gifts. Her cleaner, Doris Simpson, had called with various other well-wishers from Carsely. But James and Charles were still absent.

Toni came to drive her home. They went through the gifts, only selecting a few but keeping all the cards that went with them, and told a nurse to give the rest to the old folks' home.

They were just about to leave when Roy Silver rushed in. He was wearing a black leather jacket and black leather trousers. "Just in time," he panted. "How are you?"

"A bit shaky," said Agatha, "and feeling like a freak. You can see where they shaved off some of my hair."

"I'll come home with you and look after you," said Roy importantly. "I've hired a limo."

"Oh, Roy, how very good of you. Toni, that means you'll be able to go to the office."

When they emerged on the hospital steps it was to find a battery of television and press cameras waiting for them.

Roy stepped forward. "I am Roy Silver," he said. "You know, darlings, the one that was nearly killed."

"Bastard," hissed Agatha, "you only came for the publicity. Get me back in the hospital, Toni."

"If you wait in reception," said Toni, "I'll bring my car round to the staff entrance."

They hurried back inside.

Outside, Roy tried to continue with a prepared speech, but he was drowned out with reporters' demands to speak to Agatha.

As Toni drove off to Carsely, Agatha, still weak from medication and her injury, began to cry. "Oh, don't," pleaded Toni. "I'll soon have you home."

"James and Charles didn't even bother to come," sobbed Agatha, "and that wretched Roy only wanted publicity for himself."

"To hell with them," said Toni. "Think of all the people who came to see you and who do care about you."

Agatha dried her eyes and stared grimly through the windscreen.

Finally, Toni turned into the steep road leading down into Carsely. She drove round a bend and then put on the brakes. "What on earth . . . ?"

The village band was blocking the road. The bandmaster walked forward and peered into the car. "Welcome home," he shouted. "Follow us."

Bewildered, Agatha watched as Toni slowly followed the band. They played "When the Saints Go Marching In" as they proceeded down into Carsely. Villagers, clapping and cheering, lined the streets when they arrived in the village.

They followed the band into Lilac Lane and up to Agatha's cottage. James and Charles stood on either side of her cottage door, each holding an enormous bouquet of flowers.

"There you are!" laughed Toni. "Still feeling unloved?"

Several of the more experienced pressmen had raced from the hospital, guessing that Agatha might escape the back way. Trying not to cry, this time with gratitude, Agatha made a brief speech of thanks to the village before going inside with Toni, James and Charles. Mrs. Bloxby was waiting in the kitchen where a splendid afternoon tea was laid out on the table.

"You arranged all this," said Agatha to James and Charles. "Most of the time, the villagers think I'm the grim reaper."

"Wanted to surprise you," said Charles. "Sit down, have tea and tell us all about it."

Agatha's cats actually climbed on her lap. She stroked their soft fur and told everyone what Bill had said.

When she had finished, James said, "What misery that horrible woman has caused. The scandal of Sam, Clarice and Henry Bruce will all come out at the trial. Moses Green might lose his licence. And goodness knows what else she found out to blackmail some of the other villagers into silence."

There were frequent rings of the doorbell as more press arrived. Then Roy's voice could be heard shouting through the letterbox. "Let me in!"

"Leave him," said Agatha. "He only turned up hoping for some publicity for his precious little self."

"It's difficult," said Mrs. Bloxby. "He did nearly get killed working for you, Mrs. Raisin."

"I can't be bothered with him at the moment," said Agatha.

"I'll send him off," said Charles, "and tell him to come down another time."

They heard Charles open the door to the clamour of the press and the pleadings of Roy. Charles shut the front door behind him and cut off the noise.

"Did Bill say anything about Brian Summer?" asked James.

"Oh, do let her have her tea in peace," urged Mrs. Bloxby.

"It's all right," said Agatha. "I can talk and eat. It seems as if Mrs. Tripp delighted in manipulating him and sent him that book. The poor man is still in the psychiatric unit at Warnford Hospital. Bill wonders how she found out about the epileptic fits."

"After Bill had taken my statement," said James, "he said that Ada White confessed to having consulted Mrs. Tripp to see if she had any brew that would help the man with his fits. She recommended the magic mushrooms and told her where to find them."

"What are magic mushrooms?" asked Mrs. Bloxby.

"They're hallucinogenic and can be found in the fields," said Toni. "They're called shrooms on the street."

"She should go down in history as the Witch of Piddlebury," said Agatha.

A week went by, a week in which Mrs. Tripp did not receive any visitors, apart from her lawyer. She had tried to phone various villagers to berate them for abandoning her in her "hour of need." But both in their different ways had told her to rot in hell.

So she was delighted and surprised to be told she had a visitor. She was put into a room furnished only with a scarred wooden table and two hard chairs.

A woman, almost as old as herself, shuffled into the room. She was dressed entirely in black. She was stooped and wrinkled and wearing a red wig. "Don't you remember me, Gladys," she said. "It's me—Rosie Blacksmith."

"Rosie! Where have you been all these years?"

"Went to stay with my daughter in Canada. Came back. Thought I'd rather die alone than die of boredom. Great churchgoer, my Elsie."

"What happened to our coven that used to meet up in Quarry Hill?"

"You must have heard. Mind you, it must be about thirty years ago. Someone snuck up on us and took photos. They appeared in the *Daily Express*. There we all were, buck naked. We were a laughingstock. Folks are right cruel. Why did you leave us?"

"I had other fish to fry. Got tired of freezing my assets off and dancing around. So here I am. And I wouldn't be here if it hadn't been for that cow of a detective, Agatha Raisin."

"Do you want me to put a curse on her?" asked Rosie.

"What about killing her?"

"I'd do it for you, Gladys, for old times' sake, but I don't want to end up in here."

"You could slip something in her drink. I read the local papers. There's a Christmas fair in Ancombe this coming Saturday. Ancombe's near her village."

"It's miles off to Christmas!"

"Folks like to get their presents early."

"So what's it got to do with me, Gladys?"

"Do you still tell fortunes at fairs?"

"Yes, but not so much. My arthritis is wicked these days."

"You could offer your services, all money to go to charity. I'm good at reading people. I bet she consults you. That one's man-hungry, I'll bet. Sad sacks like her are always looking for Mr. Right."

"I can't very well offer her a drink. She's hardly likely to take one from me without getting suspicious."

"Put something in a syringe and jab her. Remember Sarah, the mad vet, who used to be one of us? Know where she is?"

The wrinkles on Rosie's face bunched up as she thought hard. "Let me see, Sarah Drinkwater. I'll need to check."

"If you get her, try to get some stuff for putting down animals."

Rosie handed a carrier bag over to Mrs. Tripp. "It's one of those special jackets. I'm allowed to give it to you. They checked it out."

Mrs. Tripp's eyes glistened with grateful tears. "That's great. I thought everyone had forgotten me."

"We never forget, do we?" said Rosie. "Give me a description of Agatha Raisin."

Rosie lived in what had once been an agricultural worker's cottage up on the outskirts of Snowshill. She paid off the taxi without giving a tip. Her cottage, unlike others, had not been modernised apart for the addition of an inside toilet. The outside was of red brick. Inside was dark and dingy.

She went to the drawers of an old rolltop desk in her living room and took out a battered notebook and thumbed through the pages.

She found an address and telephone number for

Sarah in Broadway. She dialled the number. A woman answered. "I would like to speak to Sarah," said Rosie.

"If it's my grandmother you want, she's in a home in Broadway."

"I'm an old friend. I'd like to visit her. Which home?"

"It's called the Resting Place."

Rosie rang off. She took a note of the retirement home's address. She decided it was near enough to get there on her mobility scooter and save the expense of another taxi fare.

Autumn leaves swirling about her, crouched over the handlebars, she set off down the hill to Broadway. Two women watched her go past. "Doesn't she look sinister," said one. "Just like a witch. You can just picture her on a broomstick."

Rose located the retirement home and drove up the short drive. She could only hope Sarah had retained all her wits.

Sarah Drinkwater was very fat. She had a great round face on top of several chins and seemed to be wedged into the armchair by the window in her room.

"I could hardly believe it when I heard that nurse introduce you," said Sarah. "I thought you'd be dead by now."

"Alive and kicking," said Rosie. "I need your help."

Sarah listened enthralled as Rosie described seeing Gladys Tripp. "Well, I never!" she exclaimed when Rosie had finished her tale.

"But I don't see how you can do anything," said Rosie. "It must be ages now since you'd got a practise."

"Was struck off years ago," said Sarah.

"Why?"

"I had a bad turn, a bit of a breakdown. I began to hate those damned cats and dogs and their owners slobbering over them. So I began to put a lot of them down. End of story."

Rosie looked round the comfortable room. "You've done well for yourself. These places cost a mint."

"My daughter married a very rich man. Clothing manufacturer. Left her a pile. He died suddenly." She gave a cackle of laughter.

"Heart attack?"

"How did you guess? But I kept some stuff. Bring me over that brown wooden box."

Rosie got painfully to her feet. She carried the box to Sarah and placed it on her ample lap. Sarah fished in her bosom and drew out a small key on a chain and unlocked the box.

She held up a bottle. "This is Oblivon. Kills instantly. Remember that vet over in Carsely got done for murder because he used this to bump someone off? That Agatha Raisin solved the case."

"That woman really is a pest," said Rosie.

"You can have this. No one knows I've got it. They don't search our belongings here."

Rosie returned to her cottage, took out the press cutting she had kept and phoned the organisers of the fair at Ancombe and offered her services, which they were delighted to accept, particularly when she said she would donate any money she made to Help the Aged.

Of course, if Agatha did not turn up, she'd need to find another way to get at her. One had to stand behind old friends.

Agatha was one of those people who ended up buying Christmas presents at the last minute. And after her history of several disastrous Christmases, she had no intention of going to the fair.

But on the Saturday morning, Roy Silver arrived on her doorstep, bearing a large bouquet of roses. "I'm ever so sorry, Agatha," he said.

"Oh, come in," said Agatha, taking the flowers from him, and reflecting that it was a sad day when she was glad to see Roy. But James had gone off on his travels again and Charles had disappeared in his catlike way, although unlike the Cheshire one, not even leaving a smile behind.

While Agatha put the flowers in water, Roy chattered

away about his life in the public relations business. Then he said, "On my way down here, I saw a poster advertising a Christmas fair in Ancombe."

"Christmas!" howled Agatha. "The whole thing starts earlier every year. I remember that Bible story about Jesus driving the traders away from the temple. What would He do now?"

"Don't know and don't care," said Roy huffily. "I'd like to go. There's probably lots of country things. More original than anything I could get in London."

"I suppose I'd better do something to keep you amused," said Agatha. "I'll phone Mrs. Bloxby. Maybe she'd like a lift." But Mrs. Bloxby said she had too much parish work.

Charles Fraith suddenly decided to go and see Agatha. He had gone to a dinner party the evening before and had found himself bored. Agatha could be infuriating, but no one could ever say she was boring. Finding her cottage deserted, he headed off to the vicarage, where Mrs. Bloxby told him Agatha had gone to the fair at Ancombe.

Agatha's feet hurt. Roy was an eager shopper. He bought wooden salad bowls and baskets of homemade jam, six Country Cookery Books, two sweaters, and four scarves. He was heading off to the car park with his latest purchases when Agatha noticed the fortune-teller's tent.

When Roy came back, Agatha said, "I think I'll get my fortune told."

"You don't believe that stuff," said Roy.

"It'll amuse me."

"You'll find me in the beer tent," said Roy.

Agatha had to wait in line because the fortune-teller seemed to be doing good business. Outside a sign said: MADAM ZORESTY. FORTUNES TOLD. At last it was her turn. She entered the small, dark tent.

Agatha saw an old woman sitting at a table. On the table was a pack of tarot cards and a crystal ball. The tent was dark. The fortune-teller was dressed in black velvet and with a black veil covering her head. Rosie studied her latest client and her heart began to beat with excitement. Agatha Raisin at last!

"Sit down and give me your hand," said Rosie. As Rosie held her hand, Agatha experienced an odd frisson of fear. It seemed as if the air around her was malignant.

"Yes," crooned Rosie. "You've been married twice before. I see a lot of death in your life."

Agatha said, "I came to find out about my future. I know my past."

The grip on her hand tightened. "You will not live very long."

Agatha jerked her hand away. "What?"

"Perhaps I am not seeing clearly," said Rosie. "Wait there and I will get the tarot cards."

She shuffled off into the darkness of the tent. "Bollocks," muttered Agatha and walked outside, glad to get away.

Rosie returned with the small phial of Oblivon and the syringe concealed in one of her pockets to find that Agatha had left. The tent flap opened and another woman came in, eager to have her fortune told.

"Finished for the day, dear," said Rosie. "Too tired to do any more readings."

When the woman had left, Rosie quickly put her paraphernalia into a travel bag. The fair organisers had supplied the tent. Into the bag went the crystal ball, made of plastic, the tarot cards and her black veil. She also took the takings. Help the Aged to Rosie meant helping herself. She opened a back flap of the tent, put the bag in the front of her mobility scooter and set off out of the fairground, bumping over the tussocky grass.

Charles found Agatha and Roy in the beer tent. "Oh, Charles," cried Agatha when she saw him. "You'll never guess what happened."

She told him about her weird encounter with the fortune-teller.

"Maybe she's a friend of Mrs. Tripp," said Charles. "Maybe it's her idea of giving you a scare."

"I'm going back there," said Agatha.

But when they got to the tent, several women outside told them that the fortune-teller had left. Agatha got the name of the woman who was organising the fair, a Mrs. Dolores Vine.

"She phoned us with her offer," said Dolores, a capable-looking woman. "She was offering her services free and said she would give any money to us to pass on to Help the Aged."

"What name did she give?"

"Wait a minute. I have a note of it somewhere." Dolores opened a capacious handbag and took out a notebook. "Let me see, it will be under 'volunteers.' Ah, here it is. Madam Zoresty, Ninety-five Greenway Road, Blockley."

"But Madam Zoresty can't be her real name," said Agatha.

"I'm afraid we didn't check up on her. She was offering to do it for free."

Agatha left her car at her cottage and then she and Roy got into Charles's car and they all set off for Blockley.

Blockley is a pretty village set deep in the folds of the Cotswold Hills. Greenway Road had council houses, a doctor's surgery and a few private houses but number ninety-five did not exist.

"I wonder if this mysterious visitor called on Mrs. Tripp in prison." Agatha phoned Patrick Mulligan and asked about prison visits.

"She hasn't been convicted yet," said Patrick. "She's on remand so someone who wants to see her just needs to phone the prison and arrange a visit. But whoever it is needs to show some form of identification. You'll need to see the governor at Mircester Women's Prison."

They drove to the prison. "With my luck the governor won't be there on Saturday," said Agatha. But the governor, a Mrs. Worthing, was there and agreed to see them.

She was a sturdy woman with close-cropped grey hair. "I was interested to meet you, Mrs. Raisin," she said. She glanced with disfavour at Roy in his black leather outfit and with his hair gelled into spikes. "Are you helping disadvantaged youth?"

"No," said Agatha, wishing for the hundredth time

that Roy would wear something more conservative. "This is a former colleague of mine who is staying for the week-end. And may I introduce Sir Charles Fraith."

"Sit down, then, and tell me more about the reason for your visit."

Agatha once more that day described her experience in the fortune-teller's tent. She then asked if Gladys Tripp had received any visitors.

"Let me look." She switched on a computer on her desk. "When would this visit have taken place?"

"I don't know exactly," said Agatha. "Pretty recently, possibly."

"Ah, here we are. Apart from the prison chaplain, Mrs. Tripp had one visitor, Rose Blacksmith."

"What address did she give?"

"I am afraid I cannot release that information."

The door crashed open and a wardress stood there. "Prisoner in cell twelve has hanged herself."

Mrs. Worthing gave an exclamation of dismay. She rushed to the door, shouting over her shoulder, "See yourselves out."

"She's left the computer on," said Charles, nipping round to the other side of the desk. "Quick! Take a note of this. Ivy Cottage, Church Road, Snowshill."

Roy had never quite got over the fright caused by the attempt on his life. He suddenly did not want to go on any more possibly dangerous adventures, despite the lure of publicity. "I'm feeling tired," he said when they were outside the prison. "I'm handling a big account. I should really get back to London."

"All right," said Agatha. "You came in your car, didn't you?"

"Yes."

"Okay, we'll drop you off."

Agatha was silent as Charles drove them towards Broadway. But when he reached the top of Fish Hill, she said, "I hope the old woman can't see the future."

"Cheer up," said Charles. "No fortune-teller is going to tell a client that they're soon going to die."

As they drove down Fish Hill in the gathering darkness, coloured autumn leaves swirled across the road.

"I hate this time of year," said Agatha. "I hate to see the trees dying."

"I thought you were a townie at heart," said Charles. "Townies never really pay much attention to the changing seasons."

"Maybe I've got countrified," said Agatha gloomily. "My heart is made of tweed."

"Harris or Irish?"

"Something dark and knobbly," said Agatha.

They swung off the High Street in Broadway and into Church Road. Charles drove slowly, looking to right and left. There was no sign of Ivy Cottage.

"It must be around here somewhere," said Agatha. "She must have had to produce genuine identification."

"And maybe this Rose is innocent," said Charles. "Want to call it a day?"

"No," said Agatha. "Stop the car, I'm going to knock at a few doors and see if anyone's heard of Ivy Cottage."

Charles watched Agatha with affection as she went from door to door. He admired her tenacity. He felt he ought to help her and was lazily thinking of doing just that when Agatha returned. "Got it!" she said triumphantly. "There's an old farm track a few yards up on the left."

Charles located the track and drove up. "That must be it," he said, pointing to the dark shape of an isolated cottage on the top of a hill.

He parked outside and they both climbed out of the car. "Here goes," said Agatha. She marched up to the door and rang the bell.

A dirty lace curtain twitched at one of the windows.

Then there was silence. Agatha rang the bell again and kicked the door. "Open up!" she yelled.

She heard the sound of shuffling footsteps and the door creaked open.

"Remember me?" said Agatha.

"What do you want?"

"You're a friend of Mrs. Tripp. You visited her and then told me I was shortly going to die."

Rosie peered past Agatha. "Who's that?"

"Sir Charles Fraith."

Rosie quailed. Surely she couldn't kill both of them. How could she get rid of the bodies? Agatha had probably told people where she was going. If she and her friend went missing, she, Rosie, would be a prime suspect. Her eyes filled with tears. Although she had not seen Gladys Tripp in years, the bonds of the old coven were strong. She would have to try to murder them.

"Come in," she said, turning and shuffling off.

They followed her into a small dark room crammed with furniture. It smelled of joss. "Sit down," said Rosie. "I'll just get myself a glass of water."

When she had shuffled out of the room, Agatha kicked off her shoes and silently went off to see what she was up to. In the kitchen, she saw Rosie take a syringe and a small phial out of a cupboard.

"If you're thinking of stabbing me with that, think again," said Agatha loudly.

Rosie let out a shriek of fear. She clutched the ampoule, which broke in her hand. She stared down at her hand.

"I'm calling the police," said Agatha. She went back to Charles and told him rapidly what she had found.

"You shouldn't have left her alone," said Charles. "Let's get back in there and tie her up or something."

They hurried back to the kitchen. Rosie lay slumped on the floor.

"Feel her pulse," said Charles.

"You feel it," said Agatha. "She might be faking."

With a sense of distaste, Charles felt for a pulse and found none.

"Dead as a doornail," he said, straightening up. "Whatever she meant to stab you with was lethal and fast-acting. Call the police now."

Inspector Wilkes was furious when he arrived at the cottage and got Agatha's preliminary statement. He felt that Agatha was making the police force in general and himself in particular look like a bunch of amateurs.

While a forensic team and a pathologist got to work inside the cottage, Agatha and Charles were told to go to police headquarters and wait to be questioned. In the car, Agatha said urgently, "We must get our stories straight. We must not say we got her address off the governor's computer."

"We'll say we followed her from the fair," said Charles.

"Won't do. They might hear about Roy and question him. It's no use priming Roy. He'll get it wrong."

"I know," said Charles. "We decided to go to Broadway for dinner and had parked the car and were walking when we saw her going past in her mobility scooter and turn up Church Road. By the time we got back to the car and drove to Church Road, she had disappeared. That's when you started knocking on doors to get her address."

"That'll do," said Agatha.

Grilled by Wilkes, flanked by Bill Wong, Agatha was taken over and over her story again.

At last, she lost her temper. "Instead of thanking me for finding you another murderer, who was no doubt put up to it by Mrs. Tripp, you are treating me like a suspect."

"Calm down," snapped Wilkes. "If you had told us what you had guessed, we would have got onto it right away."

"Oh, really? And then what would have happened? Rose Blacksmith would have denied the whole thing."

"You may go now," said Wilkes coldly, "but be available for further questioning."

It was after midnight when Charles and Agatha met up in the reception of headquarters. "I'm starving," complained Charles.

"I'll fix us something at home."

"God forbid!" exclaimed Charles, who knew that Agatha's idea of cooking was microwavable frozen curry. "There's an all-night place out on the ring road."

Soon they were wolfing down large plates of sausage, bacon, eggs and chips.

"What I can't understand," said Agatha, wiping her mouth and pushing her nearly empty plate away, "is why Rose Blacksmith should go so far as to try to murder me, even if Ma Tripp put her up to it."

"Did you ever look for her name on the Internet?" asked Charles.

"Hadn't time. Let's go home and try."

In her cottage, Agatha typed the name Rose Blacksmith into her computer. "Nothing here," she said, disappointed. "Should I type in nasty, old, murdering witches and see what comes up?"

"Can't think," said Charles.

"Let's see, for the fun of it, if there are any covens around. Here we are. History of one on Quarry Hill. Ah, here we are. Report all those years ago in the *Daily Express*. People dancing around a bonfire naked. Funny article about droopy figures and how some people should never be seen naked. Here we are. Nothing on our Rose but a quote from outraged witch Sarah Drinkwater. Newspaper points out she was the vet who was struck off and put in prison for two years for killing her customers' pets. I wonder if she's still alive."

Charles seized the phone book. "There's one here in Broadway, but it isn't Sarah, it's a M. Chist-Drinkwater." He gave Agatha the number. A woman answered, complaining they had woken her up, but told them, as she had told Rosie, that she was the granddaughter and that Sarah Drinkwater was in the nursing home in Broadway.

"Let's go and see that nursing home in the morning," said Agatha.

There had been nothing yet about Rosie's death in the newspapers, so when they arrived at the nursing home, they claimed to be friends of Rose Blacksmith.

"That lady was here recently," said the nurse. Agatha's eyes gleamed, experiencing the thrill of the hunter.

They were granted permission to visit Sarah and ushered into her room.

Agatha introduced them. Sarah looked at them with small faded blue eyes, nearly buried in the heavy folds of flesh on her face.

"You had a visit recently from Rose Blacksmith," said Agatha.

"So what? She's an old friend."

"*Was* an old friend," said Agatha.

"Was?"

"She died in an attempt to murder me with something she was going to put into a syringe. Know anything about that?"

"Dear me, no. I feel faint," said Sarah. "Could you pass me that box over there?"

Charles made to pick it up, but Agatha said sharply, "Leave it. Phone the police."

Sarah closed her eyes and refused to say anything. When Bill, Alice and a policewoman arrived, Agatha met them at the entrance to the nursing home and rapidly outlined what she had discovered about Sarah.

"We'll look into it," said Bill.

Sarah refused to hand over the key so Bill asked for a hammer and smashed open the box. Putting on gloves, he examined the contents.

"Mrs. Drinkwater," said Bill. "Did you give any of these veterinary medicines to Rose Blacksmith?"

"No!" said Sarah.

"From a broken phial, it has been quickly established that Rose died of Oblivon. I see you have some phials in this box. You have no right to these medicines. You were struck off."

Sarah shut her eyes. She had always wanted to meet Gladys Tripp again. But she had never imagined the meeting would take place in prison.

Gladys Tripp was returned to her cell. She was now accused of having asked Rose Blacksmith to murder Agatha Raisin. She refused to answer any questions without her lawyer. It was only when her lawyer arrived that she learned of the failed attempt on Agatha's life and the death of Rosie. She refused to answer any questions. Her lawyer gamely said they had no proof. Mrs. Tripp was returned to her cell.

She sat on her bed, brooding. All the evil gods she had prayed to had deserted her. One wrinkled hand stroked the jacket Rosie had given her. It was made of patchwork squares of silk on a wool base.

She hammered on her cell door and demanded a glass of water. When it arrived, she sat down on the hard bed again. She sent a prayer to the Horned God. Then she wrenched the bottom button off her jacket and swallowed it.

A wardress heard the noise of Mrs. Tripp's feet drumming on the cell floor and rushed in. The old woman was arched with pain and vomiting. The wardress rang for the medical orderly, but by the time he arrived, it was too late. Mrs. Tripp was dead.

Bill Wong called on Agatha in her office the following day with the news. "I hoped she would die in prison," said Agatha. "I feel sure there are murders we don't yet know about, like poor Jerry Tarrant and Lady Craton."

"The press are having a field day," said Bill. "Suicide in the cells, witchcraft, murder and mayhem. Someone has been leaking news to the media. Have they been bothering you?"

"On and off," said Agatha. "Strange as it may seem, I don't want publicity on this one. I want to forget about the whole thing and move on. How did the old lady kill herself?"

"Rose Blacksmith had given her a jacket. One of the buttons contained cyanide. Sarah Drinkwater says that in the days of the coven, they had this belief that they should be able to end their lives when they felt like it.

Hence the idea of the poisoned buttons. What a way to die!"

"If I were like Mrs. Bloxby, I'd probably pray for her soul," said Agatha, "but being me, I hope she rots in hell or comes back as a cockroach."

Epilogue

A month later, Agatha found work at the agency had dwindled. At first she was glad to spend more time in the village, but after a week or so, began to feel restless.

When Charles arrived at her cottage one Saturday, Agatha again felt irritated by the way he walked in and out of her life when he felt like it.

"Why the sour face?" asked Charles as he dumped an overnight bag in the hall.

"Come to stay?"

"Yes."

"Do you never think of phoning first to see if it will be all right? What if I were entertaining some gorgeous man?"

"Then I would bless you and leave."

"And not care?"

"What happened about the deaths of Jerry Tarrant and Lady Craton?" asked Charles, ignoring her last question.

"Both were cremated, so no hope there. We know Mrs. Tripp had something on Moses, Sam and Clarice. But what about the rest of them? She couldn't blackmail a whole village."

"Let's go and find out," said Charles. "There's no one left to try to bump you off now."

"All right," said Agatha. "I feel like a bit of action. The agency's not getting the work these days."

"You've had a lot of publicity," said Charles, sitting down at the kitchen table and taking a cigarette out of Agatha's packet, which was lying on the table, and lighting it.

"If I ever gave up smoking, you'd have to give up as well," said Agatha. "Don't you ever buy your own? Anyway, you'd think all that publicity would have generated work."

"People might think you're too expensive," said Charles. "You need the bread-and-butter work of lost pets and children. Put an ad in the local paper, giving your rates, cheap enough to undercut the others. That should bring the work in."

"Good idea. I'll try that. Do you want lunch?"

"Not one of your famous microwave meals," said Charles. "Come on. We'll find a pub on the road there."

It was raining heavily when they set off, but as they drove down the lanes approaching the village, the sky cleared.

They had stopped for a long lunch on the road, and so it was late afternoon when they parked outside the Green Man. "The pub's still open for business," said Agatha. "I'm glad the old bat didn't manage to get it closed. I'd like a word with Jenny Soper."

"Why her?"

"She went along with this business that the murders must have been committed by a stranger. I wonder if Mrs. Tripp had anything on her."

"Where does she live?"

Agatha shuffled through her notes. "Over there. That cottage by the shop."

Jenny answered the door. She backed away slightly when she saw them. "What do you want?"

"I was wondering why so many of the villagers

went along with the fiction that the murders must have been committed by a stranger," said Agatha. "Mrs. Tripp couldn't have been blackmailing everyone."

Jenny opened the door a little wider. "Come in."

Her front parlour was as neat as a pin. A comfortable sofa and two armchairs covered in bright chintz dominated the room and a log fire was crackling on the hearth.

Charles and Agatha sat side by side on the sofa and Jenny perched on the edge of an armchair. "People used to go to her for herbal cures," said Jenny. "Last winter, I couldn't get rid of a cough and she gave me a mixture which cleared it up. She seemed harmless. We got to talking a bit. I told her about my marriage. I'm divorced now and Raph, my ex, is doing time for armed robbery."

"That surely wasn't enough to keep you quiet," said Agatha.

"She gave me some tea that made me feel warm and sleepy. I found myself confiding in her that I used to be a drug addict and all the battle I had getting off the things.

"It was shortly after you arrived that she called on me and said it would be a good idea if I put it about that it must have been a stranger. She said Peter Suncliff might change his ideas about me if he knew I used to be a drug addict married to an armed robber."

"But Mr. Suncliff is surely much older than you."

"I'm forty-two. I'm older than I look. Peter is everything my former husband isn't. He's affectionate and dependable. He told me once that drug addicts disgust him."

"If he's all that decent a man," said Charles, "your past shouldn't bother him."

"I couldn't bear the secrecy anymore," said Jenny. "Just before she was arrested I told him. He said he already knew. Mrs. Tripp told him that unless he went along with the fiction about the murderer, she'd tell everyone in the village about my past. He kept quiet for my sake. This is a closed community. People value respectability. I had carved out a new life for myself here."

"You don't work," said Agatha. "How do you manage for money?"

"My parents died just after the divorce and left me quite well off. I left Birmingham and wanted to start a new life here. Peter and I are going to be married."

"That's great," said Charles. "Is the vicar still married?"

Jenny looked at him, round-eyed. "Why wouldn't he be?"

"Silly thing to say," said Charles hurriedly. "I was thinking of some other vicar."

"I thought the police would have been round prosecuting people for impeding the police in their enquiries," said Agatha, when they left Jenny's cottage.

"I think Mrs. Tripp's death closed the case for them. What about the wicked vet?"

"Sarah died of a heart attack in prison. It was in the papers," said Agatha.

"I haven't been reading them lately. Do we really need to go around digging up everyone's nasty secrets?" said Charles. "Poor souls. It's such an odd place. Not like the Cotswold villages where newcomers are no novelty. Makes you feel you ought to set your watch back one hundred years."

"Still, let's call on Sam. I'm curious. Also, the vicar said God had told him the identity of the murderer. I want to find out if God got it right."

"Okay. Vicarage first and then Sam."

Clarice opened the vicarage door to Agatha and glared at her. She was holding a large glass of wine in one hand and a cigarette in the other, both signs the vicar was not at home.

"Piss off," she said. "One witch in a village is enough without a witch bitch like you haunting my doorstep."

The door slammed in their faces.

"I wonder what the Mother's Union makes of her?" said Charles.

"Oh, she can act the part of the vicar's lady to perfection," said Agatha. "Let's try the church."

They entered the gloom of the church. Ada White was arranging a vase of flowers by the altar. She turned and saw them, let out a shriek, dropped the vase and ran past them out of the church.

Guy Enderbury appeared from the vestry. "What was that noise? Oh, it's you."

"Ada knocked over the flowers," said Agatha.

"Dear me, what a mess," said the vicar, looking down at the shattered glass vase and the flowers lying on the floor. "I'll get our cleaner, Mrs. Pound, to clear it up."

"Did God really tell you who the murderer was?" asked Agatha.

"That is between me and my Maker."

"Meaning you didn't know, but you hoped whoever it was would come after you," said Agatha.

"You are an unbeliever," said Guy.

"Only when it comes to codswallop."

"Was Mrs. Tripp blackmailing you?" asked Charles.

"Of course not. There is nothing in my life she could blackmail me about."

"It has been said," remarked Agatha, her eyes boring into his, "that you only married the Broadway barmaid because you got her pregnant."

"Mrs. Tripp could hardly blackmail me over something that was common knowledge at the time. Get out of my church!"

Agatha itched to ask him about Henry Bruce. But what if the police had not said anything?

She and Charles reluctantly left. Guy stood in the middle of the aisle, glaring after them.

"Sam next, I suppose," said Charles. "This is all a waste of time, Agatha."

"I'm curious, that's what," said Agatha.

They made their way to the manor house, Fred answered the door and looked them up and down. "What the hell do you want?" he demanded.

"Always the perfect butler," said Agatha. "We're here to see Sam."

"Lady Framington to you."

"Tell her we're here!" shouted Agatha.

Sam appeared behind Fred. "What are you doing back here?" she demanded. "It's all over with."

"We're curious," said Agatha. "Was Mrs. Tripp blackmailing you over your affair with . . ."

"Come inside," said Sam quickly. "That voice of yours is so loud, it's like a megaphone."

They followed her into the drawing room. "I did not have an affair with anyone," said Sam.

"Not even with Henry Bruce?" said Agatha.

"I'm hardly likely to hop into bed with the hired help. Now, your friend James Lacey was another matter. Quite delicious."

"James wouldn't . . . couldn't . . ." spluttered Agatha.

"Oh, he could and did."

"Come on, Aggie," said Charles. "She'll just sit here all day, lying her head off."

James Lacey, earlier that day, had been shopping in the market in Mircester for vegetables when he came across Toni. They stood looking at each other awkwardly, and James said, "I did make such a fool of myself, Toni. Forgot my age. I am sorry."

"Oh, I was just as much to blame," said Toni with a shy smile.

"Look, it's lunchtime. Join me?"

"Why not?" They walked out of the square and along to the George Hotel.

The day was dark and the lights were on in the dining room. After they had sat down, James noticed a small diamond ring glittering on Toni's engagement finger.

He pointed to the ring. "Is that what I think it is?"

"Yes, it is," said Toni. "I've met someone at last."

"Not as old as I am, I hope," said James.

"He's a medical student," said Toni. "His name is Frank Evans. He's two years older than I am."

"That's a blessing. Got a photo?"

Toni smiled. "Of course."

She fished in her handbag and drew out a photo and handed it to James. It showed a very handsome young man with dark curly hair and hazel eyes.

"When's the wedding?"

"We're going to wait until Frank gets his degree. We're looking for a flat. Mine is too small."

"Doesn't Frank have a bigger flat?"

"No, his is as small as mine."

"What do his parents think of the engagement?"

"His father is dead. I'm meeting his mother for dinner tonight. She's travelling up from Wales."

"And does Agatha know?" asked James.

"Not yet. Anyway, my private life is none of her business."

"Let's order and then you can tell me more."

Once the waiter had taken their orders, Toni said,

"I met him at a pop concert. Some youths were annoying me and he stepped in. We went for a drink."

"When was this?"

"A week ago."

James wanted to say that surely that was a bit rushed, but felt that he, of all people, had the least right to question Toni's happiness. As the meal went on, he could only be glad that he and Toni seemed to have returned to their former easy-going relationship.

"Don't be nervous," Frank said to Toni that evening. "Mother will adore you. And you'll adore her. She's so bright and clever and friendly. I've booked a table at the George."

Toni had not seen a photograph of Frank's mother and imagined she would be a plump Welshwoman with rosy cheeks, black hair, and a lilting voice.

The real woman came as a shock. Mrs. Evans was a thin dyed blonde with a wind-tunnel facelift and a mouth enhanced by collagen. That mouth was painted scarlet and seemed to hang on her thin white face as if it did not belong to it.

Frank embraced her and she clung on to him fiercely. Then she released him and her pale eyes raked up and down Toni. "So this is your little friend?"

"Yes, this is Toni."

"I assume that's sort for Antonia."

"No," said Toni. "I was christened Toni with an i, not y."

"Dear me, the odd names they do give girls these days."

They sat down at a table at the window. The waiter came up and Mrs. Evans ordered a martini, Frank had the same, and Toni ordered sparkling mineral water.

Mrs. Evans came from Cardiff. She and her son promptly launched into a conversation about people Toni didn't know, Frank laughing uproariously at all his mother's anecdotes. The rain, which had ceased earlier, began to fall again.

This is awful, thought Toni, gazing bleakly at the rain smearing the plate-glass windows. I wish I were like Mrs. Bloxby and believed in God and I could ask for divine help to get me out of this.

"Toni!" cried a familiar voice. Toni looked across the dining room. Agatha and Charles were bearing down on their table.

Toni made the introductions. "Your fiancé?" said Agatha. "When did all this happen?"

"About a week ago."

"Marry in haste, repent at leisure, is what I always say," remarked Mrs. Evans. "Don't want my precious just throwing himself away on anyone."

"Then he's damned lucky he's got a pearl like Toni,"

said Agatha. She signalled to the headwaiter. "This is a celebration. Move us all to a bigger table and bring champagne."

Charles whispered in her ear. "You're butting in, Agatha."

"She needs help," muttered Agatha.

After the food was ordered and the champagne poured, Agatha got to her feet. "Here's to Toni Gilmour," she said. "The best detective ever."

"Such an odd job for a little girl," said Mrs. Evans. She turned to her son when the toast was over and picked up her conversation with him where she had left off.

Agatha said to Toni, "We've just been to Piddlebury."

"Did you find out why they all banded together with this fiction that the murders were done by an outsider?" asked Toni.

"Stonewalled at every turn," said Charles, "apart from Jenny Soper, who admitted to being blackmailed. Such an odd village. So closed in. I bet there was a lot of incest in the old days."

Mrs. Evans found to her annoyance that her son was no longer listening to her. "Are you all right now?" Frank asked Agatha. "Toni told me you got struck on the head and then the murderers tried to push you down the well."

Agatha launched into a highly colourful, highly embroidered account of her adventures, pausing only to eat her food.

Frank was now not even pretending to listen to his mother.

Mrs. Evans couldn't bear it. She interrupted Agatha and said in a high, thin voice, "I hope Toni is not going to continue with this unsavoury work after she is married."

"I need to make a living," protested Toni.

"But there are more suitable jobs. I happen to have a friend who owns a florist's shop in Mircester. Now, there's a *genteel* job for you."

"Why don't you take it yourself," said Agatha. "Don't have a job, do you?"

"My poor Ethelred left me very comfortably off, thank you."

Agatha cackled with laughter. "Poor man. Did he get called Ethel at school?"

Mrs. Evans threw her napkin down on the table. "I've had enough of this. I feel faint. Help me out, Frank."

"I'll phone you later, Toni," said Frank.

Agatha, Charles and Toni watched as Mrs. Evans, clutching onto her son, left the dining room.

Toni got to her feet. "Agatha, couldn't you just, this one evening, mind your own business?"

Charles looked at Agatha's downcast face. "Cheer up," he said. "Toni will come to her senses. That damned mother of his will win out in the end."

But the next morning when Agatha arrived in the office, it was to find Toni waiting for her. Grim-faced, Toni said, "I'm giving you a month's notice. You nearly ruined my engagement."

"Look, I'm sorry," pleaded Agatha. "But the woman was insufferable."

"Did it never dawn on you that I might be able to cope?" asked Toni. "I am not a child."

"But where will you go? What will you do?"

"I shall join the police force."

"Oh, Toni. Please stay. We can't do without you."

"You should have thought of that. Now, I'm off to work on the Bryelys' divorce case."

She went out and slammed the door.

Agatha went to the window and stared down into the street. Toni emerged and walked towards the car park. Before she turned the corner, she gave a little skip, like someone who has found freedom at last.

Phil put an arm around Agatha's shoulders. "Don't worry," he said. "She'll change her mind."

But the month passed and Toni showed no signs of relenting. Agatha decided to give a farewell party for her in the office. The staff arrived early, the champagne was in two ice buckets and canapés laid out on the desks. Patrick, Simon, Phil, Mrs. Freedman and Agatha had all bought presents.

The clock on the wall ticked past nine o'clock. No sign of Toni. "Check your e-mail," said Phil. "Maybe she's ill."

"She would surely have phoned." But Agatha checked her e-mail. There was one from Toni.

Agatha read, "I couldn't bear the idea of the last day so I've gone off to Wales with Frank to visit his mother. Thanks for everything. Toni."

In a faltering voice, Agatha read it aloud.

"This is all your fault," yelled Simon, who had received an account of that disastrous dinner from Toni. "Well, you can damn well take my notice as well."

They all stared at him as he crossed the office and slammed the door behind him.

Agatha sat staring at her computer. "I don't know about you," said Patrick. "But I could do with a drink. Come on, Agatha. Let's all get pissed."

He cracked open a bottle of champagne and began to fill glasses.

He raised his glass. "Here's to Agatha Raisin. The best detective in the world."

That was when the usually indomitable Agatha began to cry.

A week later, Phil took a large box with all the presents round to Toni's flat. When she opened the door, he handed her the box. "Presents for you," he said.

"Bring them in," said Toni in a subdued voice.

Phil placed them on the floor. "Coffee?" asked Toni.

"No, thanks," said Phil. "I've got to get back to work. Congratulations, by the way. You've finally made our Agatha cry."

Toni coloured up. "I'm a free spirit, Phil. It's my life. I can leave if I want to."

"Look, she arranged a farewell party for you, we all brought these presents, and all you do is send an e-mail."

Toni hung her head. "I'll apologise."

"Don't do that. Keep clear and let her forget about the whole thing. Simon has left as well. We've got a lot of work to do. Goodbye, Toni."

After he had left, Toni opened her presents. Agatha had given her a box of Chanel cosmetics; Phil, a book token; Patrick, a guidebook on police work; Mrs. Freedman, a box of embroidered handkerchiefs; and Simon, a large bottle of Dior perfume.

She sat there for a long time, reflecting on the quite horrible week she had spent in Cardiff. Toni felt more trapped now by Mrs. Evans than she had ever felt with Agatha. For Mrs. Evans had it all worked out. Toni and Frank were to have an early wedding and come and live with her in her bungalow, called Mon Repos. Frank would transfer his studies to Cardiff and Toni could find suitable work. Toni and Frank had had a painful row, Frank thinking the arrangement was a good one. The engagement was still on but she and Frank had parted on strained terms. How much in love I was, thought Toni, remembering the days when she was encased in a golden bubble. Now, the bubble had burst and she did not know what to do.

At last she phoned Bill Wong and made an arrangement to meet him and ask his advice about joining the police, even though Bill, too, had an awful mother in whom he could never see any faults.

They met in a pub near Bill's home that evening. He listened carefully to the whole saga even though he had already heard a lot of it from Agatha. He squirmed a little as her soft voice went on, remembering the times when his own mother had told his latest romance that she and Bill would live with his parents and how his latest love had melted away. When she had finished, he said cautiously, "You had a lot of freedom working for Agatha. There's tight discipline in the police force. Because of the rules about taking on ethnic minorities, you'd probably not get a job in Mircester. Then when you do qualify, you'll start at the bottom, traffic control and things like that. Also, the police can be pretty sexist. We're not bad in Mircester, but some stations, I believe, can be pretty rough for a woman. Where is Simon?"

"He's gone to work for one of Agatha's rivals."

"Poor Agatha. What a mess. Is Mrs. Evans really as awful as she said?"

"Worse."

"Engagement still on?"

"Just."

"My advice is to go back to Agatha and ask for your job back."

"I can't do that! I didn't turn up for the farewell party and they had presents for me."

"I think Agatha has a bigger heart than you give her credit for."

That evening, Agatha was saying to Mrs. Bloxby, "I've told you. I wouldn't take that ungrateful little girl back if she came crawling on her knees."

There was a silence while the vicar's wife sipped sherry. Then she said, "People don't often recognise jealousy in themselves. Because if you are jealous of someone, you are in competition with them, and looking down at them at the same time. So when someone accuses you of jealousy, you're apt to say, 'Jealous of her? You must be mad. She's nothing but . . .' and so on."

"I'm not jealous of Toni," said Agatha mulishly.

"Miss Gilmour is very young. She may be feeling a bit lost, now she has possibly spent more time with the mother."

Agatha heaved a sigh. "She won't be back. Start of a new era. I'm interviewing new detectives tomorrow. I can forget about Piddlebury. Stupid people. Not one of them had the guts to go to the police. It stands to reason if someone is blackmailing you into silence to tell a lie about the murderer, then that very person is probably the murderer. Sod the lot of them."

"I really don't think that village will ever be the same," said Mrs. Bloxby. "I think there will come a change for the better."

"Maybe in the next hundred years," said Agatha.

Fog was enveloping the village when Agatha trudged back to her cottage. She let herself in. Charles's lazy voice came from her living room. "In here, Aggie."

Agatha strode in. "How many times have I told you to stop calling me . . ."

Her voice trailed off. Toni was sitting by the fire. She rose to her feet and faced Agatha.

"I-I-I w-wondered if I could have my j-job back," she stammered.

Agatha stood with her head down, staring at the floor.

"Don't see why not," she said at last. "Pour me a gin and tonic, Charles, while I get my coat off."

Agatha went into the hall and hung up her damp coat. She stared at herself in the mirror.

A slow smile crossed her face.

Maybe Mrs. Bloxby is right, thought Agatha Raisin, and there is a God after all. I've got Toni back and Simon has gone. Oh, happy day.

Read on an excerpt from

The Blood of an Englishman

—the next Agatha Raisin mystery by M.C. Beaton,
available soon in hardcover from Minotaur Books!

"Fee, fie, fo, fum. I smell the blood of an Englishman."

As the giant ogre in the Winter Parva pantomime
strutted across the stage, uttering the old familiar words,
Agatha Raisin stifled a yawn. She loathed amateur
dramatics, but had been persuaded to support the
pantomime by her friend, Mrs. Bloxby, the vicar's wife.
The two women were in odd contrast: Agatha with her
smart clothes and glossy brown hair, Mrs. Bloxby in
faded tweeds and wispy brown hair streaked with grey
surrounding her gentle face.

Agatha began to feel sulky and trapped. Why was she, a private detective of some fame, wasting her sweetness on the desert air of the Winter Parva village hall?

The pantomime was *Babes In the Woods*, but there were also characters from other pantomimes from *Old Mother Hubbard* to *Puss in Boots*.

At last the interval arrived. There was no theatre bar but mulled wine was being served in the entrance hall. Agatha grabbed a glass and said, "Going outside for a cigarette."

Fog lay heavily on the car park and water dripped mournfully from the trees surrounding it. "Still smoking? Dear me," said a voice behind Agatha. She swung round and found herself looking down at the gossip of her home village, Carsely, Mrs. Arnold.

"Yes," said Agatha curtly.

"Do you know that only twenty per cent of the people in Britain now smoke?" said Mrs. Arnold.

"I never believe in statistics," said Agatha. "Have they asked everyone?" She surveyed Mrs. Arnold's small round figure. "Anyway, what about overeating? What about a ban on *fat* people?"

A tall man loomed up out of the mist. "What do you think of the show?"

Agatha bit back the word "hellish" that had risen to her lips and said instead, "I think the chap playing the ogre is very good. Who is he?"

"That's our local baker, Bert Simple. I haven't introduced myself. I recognise you. I'm Gareth Craven, producer of the show. That's the end of the interval. I'd better get backstage."

"I'm Agatha Raisin," Agatha called after him.

Quite tasty, thought Agatha, watching his tall figure disappear into the fog. Well, hullo hormones, I thought you had laid down and died.

She shuffled along her seat besides Mrs. Bloxby. The hall smelled of damp people, mulled wine, and chocolates. A surprising number had brought boxes of chocolates. Pen lights flickered, voices murmured things like, "I don't want a hard one. Are those liqueur chocolates, you naughty man!" Children, used to slumping on comfortable sofas in front of the television, screamed and hit each other.

The curtains were drawn back and the comedian came on. "Hullo, hullo, hullo!" he yelled.

"Goodbye, goodbye, goodbye," muttered Agatha.

The comedian was a local man, George Southern, who owned a gift shop in the village.

He was slightly built and rather camp with thin brown hair and a large nose which overshadowed his small mouth.

"I hope you're in good voice tonight, folks," he said.

A screen came down behind him. It's the compulsory singalong, thought Agatha bleakly.

Sure enough. The words of *It's a Long Way to Piccadilly* appeared on the screen. Why an old First World War song, wondered Agatha. and then came to the conclusion that they were possibly frightened that anything more modern would incur royalties. From previous experience, she knew that amateur dramatic companies seemed to think the eyes of the world were on them. It seemed to go on forever. He got the men to sing, then the women, then the children. "Follow the bouncing ball," he yelled, strutting about the stage in his moment of glory.

The curtains were drawn again and opened to reveal a cardboard cottage. The Babes were played by two ill-favoured children, who turned out to be the son and daughter of the head of the parish council, which was why they had landed the parts.

"Here comes the ogre again," said Mrs. Bloxby.

"Isn't there supposed to be a witch?" said Agatha.

"Shhh!" admonished a voice behind them.

"Fee! Fie! Fo! Fum! I smell the blood of an Englishman," roared Bert. "Be he alive, or be he dead, I'll grind his bones to make my bread."

He was a burly man with a big round head and small glittering eyes, wearing built-up boots to make him look like a giant.

Slowly descending on a creaking wire came the Good Fairy. It broke when she was nearly down and she fell on a heap on the stage. "Can't you bloody bastards do anything properly?" she yelled. The children whistled and cheered.

"Shame!" called a voice from the audience. "Remember the children."

The Good Fairy rallied, picked up her bent wand and faced the ogre. "I am banishing you to the pit from whence you came," she said.

There was an impressive puff of green smoke. A trap door opened and Bert disappeared. The small orchestra started to play a jolly tune. A chorus line-up of ill-assorted tap dancers thudded their way across the stage. The pantomime dragged on to the close. At the final curtain, there was no sign of Bert.

"It was all right, considering it was an amateur show," ventured Mrs. Bloxby,

Agatha bit back the nasty remark that was rising to her lips. The two women had come in their separate cars. She said goodnight to her friend, warning her to drive carefully, because the fog was even thicker.

As Agatha was nearing Carsely, police cars heading for Winter Parva raced past on the other side of the road. Agatha did a u-turn and followed them. "Something's up," she muttered. "Maybe someone's murdered that dreadful comedian."

Soon she could see flashing blue lights outside the village hall.

The thick mist meant she was able to get into the car park before the police taped off the area. Where was the stage door? That chap, Gareth, had left and gone round the side of the building.

She walked to the building and found a small door, standing open. A policeman supporting Gareth Craven came along a corridor inside. "If I could just get some fresh air," said Gareth. His face was chalk white.

Agatha stepped boldly forward. "I'm a friend of Mr. Craven," she said. "I'll look after him. You can come out when you're ready and take a statement. I have a Peugeot parked outside."

"Name?"

"Mrs. Bloxby," said Agatha, fearing that the sound of her own name would alert the fact to the policeman that she was a private detective.

"Registration number of your car?"

Agatha gave it to him and then put an arm around Gareth's waist. "Come along," she said. "I've some brandy in the car."

"I thought you were Agatha Raisin," said Gareth.

"I am," said Agatha, "but I didn't want that policeman to know that. Here we are. In you go and I'll get the heater on."

Once Gareth was settled in the passenger seat and had taken a few swigs of brandy from a flask Agatha kept in the car, Agatha said, "What happened in there?"

"It was awful," said Gareth. "When Bert didn't appear for the curtain call, I went back to look for him. He wasn't in any of the dressing rooms. I went down under the platform and there he was. Oh, God!"

He buried his face in his hands. Agatha waited until she thought he had recovered and said, "Go on. What happened to him?"

"He was standing there, very still, his mouth opened in a sort of awful silent scream. There was a big pool of blood at his feet. I couldn't find a pulse. I ran upstairs and phoned police, ambulance and fire brigade. The lot. I couldn't bear any more. That's it."

There was a peremptory rap on the car window. Agatha lowered it and found Detective Sergeant Bill Wong staring accusingly at her. "I'll speak to you later," he said. "Mr. Craven. Please come with me. We need a statement. And Mrs. Raisin, please drive your car beyond the taped-off police area."

Bill must be really cross to call me Mrs. Raisin, thought Agatha. The young detective was the first friend she ever made when she came to the Cotswolds.

She decided to drive home and wait for the news the following day. Whatever had happened to Bert, it would be too late for the morning papers, but there might be something on television. But if it were an accident, then nothing would appear at all.

She was to get the news from an unexpected quarter.

The following day was Sunday. Agatha contemplated making one of her rare visits to morning service, thought better of it, turned over and went back to sleep.

She did not get up until mid-day. She rose, dressed and went down to feed her cats, Hodge and Boswell, and let them out into the garden. An icy wind was blowing. Both cats turned on the threshold and looked up at her.

"Go on," urged Agatha. "You've got fur coats on, haven't you?"

Just then, the front doorbell rang. When Agatha opened the door, it was to find a tired-looking Mrs. Bloxby on the step.

"It's awful," said the vicar's wife.

"Come in," said Agatha. "I'll put the coffee on."

She waited until her friend was seated at the kitchen table with a mug of coffee, and asked, "What's going on?"

"I've been out a good part of last night. Mrs. Simple was in a terrible state. She asked to speak to Alf." Alf was the vicar. "We both went to Winter Parva. The doctor had been called and had given Mrs. Simple a tranquilliser but she was still in a state. She said God was punishing her for being a bad wife."

"Was Bert's death murder? Was she saying she killed him?" asked Agatha.

"No, not at all. But it appears to have been a particularly vicious murder. And well thought-out, too. A small square had been cut out of the elevator platform. Evidently it always descended a bit too quickly and landed with a bump. Well, when Mr. Simple descended, a long steel spike had been embedded in the floor so that it went up through the hole in the platform, right between his legs and up into his body. Alf and I managed to persuade Mrs. Simple to go to bed and we sat and talked quietly to her until she fell asleep."

"Doesn't Winter Parva have a vicar?"

"No, Alf takes services there twice a month."

"Wait a bit," said Agatha. "I don't get this. How on earth would anyone have time to fix that spike and not be discovered?"

"Mr. Simple was killed the first time he descended. That was towards the end of the pantomime. Evidently he had been complaining about the speed it went down and said he would only do it the once."

"But there would be a dress rehearsal!"

"I suppose so. His son, Walt, told us that no one goes down there except the blacksmith."

"Do we have blacksmiths in this day and age?"

"Yes, of course. We have three hunts around here. And Mr. Crosswith, the blacksmith, also does wrought iron gates and things. Bert had been complaining that the trap was a bit dangerous. Mr. Crosswith designed a star trap from some old Victorian drawings."

"What is a star trap?" asked Agatha.

"Star traps consist of a permanent stage floor, made up of several triangular sections of flooring meeting at the centre, which may be lifted but which naturally fall flat. Under the stage is an elevator using counterweights that are heavier than the weight of the performer.

"To make an impressive entrance, the elevator platform is first lowered, at which point a brake is applied, to stop the counterweight falling. The performer steps onto the platform. On cue, the brake is removed allowing the counterweights to fall. The performer is thrust through the star trap door. When the platform hits the highest point the performer leaps upward clearing the trap door sections, which then fall back into position at floor level. With a puff of smoke, the illusion is complete. Then in reverse, the flats open and Mr. Simple descends. Do you understand all that?"

"Sort of," said Agatha cautiously. "How do you know all this?"

"The Mother's Union was given a tour of the hall earlier this year to show how it had been used back in the Victorian days. The blacksmith gave us a lecture on the trap."

"Do you think someone tampered with the brakes so that the platform would go down extra-fast?"

"Maybe. But it went down pretty fast anyway."

"How does anyone get in under the stage? Is there an outside door?"

"You can get through under the platform at the front. I know that. But whether there is another entrance, I can't say. I know Bert only made one entrance through the trap, so it could have been tampered with any time earlier."

Agatha lit a cigarette and watched the smoke drift up towards the kitchen ceiling. "Wait a minute. In order for Bert to disappear, someone below the stage must have operated the elevator."

"I gather that the stage manager pressed a button at the side of the stage which opened the trap and sent the green smoke up."

"But the stage manager, or Gareth Craven, the producer, surely checked on the apparatus before the show."

"If things went all right at the dress rehearsal, Mrs. Raisin, maybe a check wasn't considered necessary," said Mrs. Bloxby.

We really should start to call each other by our first names, thought Agatha. We called each other by our second names in the Ladies Society. But the Society is long gone.

"What about the spike, or whatever it was that killed Bert?"

"I don't know about that. Someone must have really hated him," said Mrs. Bloxby. "Such an elaborate way of killing him!"

"The blacksmith must be the obvious culprit," said Agatha.

"I believe he is a quiet, sensitive man," said Mrs. Bloxby.

"Oh, well," said Agatha. "I'll need to leave this one to the police. I've got my own business to run and I can't see anyone in Winter Parva wanting to pay me to investigate the murder of a baker."

On a Monday morning, a week later, Agatha, as usual, greeted her staff before settling down to have her usual breakfast at her desk – one cup of strong black coffee and two cigarettes. Her staff consisted of young, blonde and beautiful Toni Gilmour, white-haired gentle Phil Marshall, lugubrious ex-policeman Patrick Mulligan, young Simon Black with his jester's face, and secretary Mrs. Freedman. Simon had left briefly to work for another agency when he thought Toni had resigned. But when he heard Toni had returned, he had promptly asked for his job back. Agatha did not like Simon much, but had rehired him in a weak moment.

Agatha blew out a smoke ring. Mrs. Freedman gave an admonitory cough and switched on an extractor fan she had insisted on having installed.

"Let's see," said Agatha. "Toni and Simon, you have Mrs. Fairly's case. She wants proof of her husband's infidelity. Phil and Patrick, you've got two missing teenagers. You've got their details and photographs?"

Both nodded.

"Right," said Agatha. "I've got Berry's supermarket. Valuable goods have been disappearing from their electronics section and so far there's been nothing on their CCTV cameras. I'm going to spend the day there."

"Someone's coming," said Toni. "Might be something interesting." Toni hoped it might be a job that she could do on her own. She did not like working with Simon. He was constantly asking her out on dates and she found it all embarrassing.

The door opened and a man Agatha recognised as Gareth Craven walked in. He was even better-looking that Agatha remembered. She did a frantic mental check. Did she have coffee-stained teeth? Had her lipstick faded? Why had she opted for trousers and flat shoes?

Gareth Craven was a tall man with thick brown hair, clear grey eyes, a firm mouth, and a handsome face which unfortunately ended in a rather weak chin.

"Please take a seat, Mr. Craven," said Agatha, thinking, nobody's perfect.

"I really need your help," said Gareth. "You see, the newspapers are after me already and they are making me feel guilty. You would think I had done it. I've stopped answering the door or the phone. Mrs. Raisin, you have such a good reputation for solving cases. I wondered if I could employ you."

"Certainly," said Agatha. "Mrs. Freedman will draw up a contract for you. I will start on it right away. Toni, you take over Berry's supermarket for me." Simon's face fell. He had been looking forward to a day with Toni.

Mrs. Freedman came over with the contracts. Gareth barely looked at the price and quickly signed them.

"Now," said Agatha to Gareth, "we'll clear off somewhere for a coffee and you can give me all the details."

In the old-fashioned gloom of the George Hotel lounge, after coffee had been served, Agatha asked, "Who, in your opinion, would want to kill Bert?"

"That's the problem," said Gareth. "I don't know where to tell you to start."

"Have you discussed it with your wife?" asked Agatha.

"I'm not married. Divorced."

"Like me," said Agatha cheerfully. "What about the blacksmith?"

"Harry Crosswith is a pillar of the community. He's in a terrible state."

"How could anyone guarantee that the spike would kill Bert? I mean, he could have been at the edge of the platform."

"It's a small platform," said Gareth, "and Bert is – was – a big man. He complained that the lift went down too fast. In fact he and Harry had a bit of a row about it. Harry was very proud of that trap."

"What about the nearest and dearest? How old is the son, Walt?"

"He's twenty. Works in the bakery. Quiet and reliable."

"And Mrs. Simple?"

Gareth's face softened. "Gwen is a saint. She works serving in the shop. Everybody loves her."

Not you, I hope, thought Agatha. Aloud she said, "Perhaps I should start today by asking some of the locals. Who's the biggest gossip in the village?"

"Well, there's Marie Tench. But she can be spiteful."

"Maybe just the sort of person I should talk to," said Agatha. "Have you her address?"

"She's got a flat above the newspaper shop opposite the old marketplace."

"I'll start there. Tell me about yourself. How did you get involved with producing this pantomime?"

"I was a producer with BBC Radio 4 for years. Last year, I was suddenly made redundant. They're cutting jobs all round. It was a bit of a blow, but I'm lucky enough to have private means so I thought I would keep my hand in by producing this pantomime."

"But it wasn't very professional, surely," said Agatha. "I mean, it was a sort of mish-mash of all the pantomime characters."

"I know. Mrs. Grant of the Women's Institute wrote the script and was to produce it, but she died. I wanted to make changes but the cast protested and said it should be kept just the way it was in her memory."

"Any friction amongst the cast?"

He sighed. "I think amateur productions are worse than professional ones for fragile egos. The Good Fairy, Pixie Turner, went on as if she had a leading role in a Shakespeare production. Then that so-called comedian was always groping the chorus girls."

"Where does the chorus line come from?"

"Winter Parva High School. They have tap dancing classes there."

"Any little Lolitas that Bert might have had his eye on?"

"Oh, no! He was devoted to his wife."

"I think I've enough names to be going on with," said Agatha. "I'll start with the village gossip and then maybe later on you can introduce me to the blacksmith if the police aren't still grilling him."